THE KNACK OF DOING

ALSO BY JEREMY M. DAVIES *Rose Alley* (2009) | *Fancy* (2015)

THE KNACK OF DOING

STORIES

JEREMY M. DAVIES

A BLACK SPARROW BOOK

DAVID R. GODINE, PUBLISHER

BOSTON

This is
A Black Sparrow Book
published in 2016 by
David R. Godine, Publisher
Post Office Box 450
Jaffrey, New Hampshire 03452
www.blacksparrowbooks.com

The Black Sparrow Books pressmark is by Julian Waters

LIBRARY OF CONGRESS CATALOGING-IN-PUBLICATION DATA
Davies, Jeremy, 1978–
[Short stories. Selections]
The knack of doing : stories / Jeremy Davies.
p. cm.
ISBN 978-1-57423-227-1 (alk. paper)
I. Title.

PS3604.A9537A6 2015
813'.6—dc23

2015024978

Cover design by Sarah French
Cover illustration by Katie So

First Edition
Printed in the United States

For Judy Esther and David Abraham Davies

And Sarah, as ever

CONTENTS

I.

FORKHEAD BOX

What interests me most is that Schaumann, the state executioner, bred mice. In his spare time. Sirens, ozone, exhaust are all words I might use to entice you into thinking yourself interested in the scene at Sing Sing where Schaumann, of whom you'll hear quite a bit more, was dispatching such and such a killer on a day, let's say, in spring. Did you know that he lived in an undecorated house? As a rule, he was inclined toward plainness. An absence of adornment in his clothing, comestibles, decorations, speech, wife, car, habits. He would have lived thus even if employed as a dogcatcher or chiropodist. He had never been otherwise. Ostentation was indefensible. He pretended not to see it. Tasteful or un, he found anything done for no reason than to excite the senses to be in poor form. Perhaps the result of a transcription error in ye old zygotic alphabet. A possibility that would not have been unfamiliar to Schaumann, breeding his mice. Here a one with a longer tail, there a one who wouldn't take food. Schaumann eschewed even condiments. Nor would he wear charms or trinkets. He had lost his wedding ring on his honeymoon. While swimming. Sucked away by the salt he would not have added to his beef stew. Leading his wife to jibe that Schaumann was now married to the sea. Yes: a joke, for those with an ear for such things. But Schaumann had no wit. Even less guile. His children found it easy to deceive him. His children found him simple. Given his profession, however, I am tempted to see something defensive in his meticulous triviality. Ostentation would draw attention. If attention were paid to Schaumann, the attender might learn what Schaumann did for a living.

So he was ashamed of it?

Sources differ.

His children found him simple. I think they were mistaken. And, anyway, they will not read this story. I won't encourage them to do so, and I'll ask that you not bring it to their attention. And did you know that when Schaumann left his house to drive to the state prison to execute someone, he changed his license plates halfway? I'm unsure as to the legality or feasibility of this. Maybe he had received some sort of dispensation from the state. I'm sure the state made allowances for the privacy of its employees engaged in such sensitive work. And that was how Schaumann lived his private life: he was one man in town, walking to the store, going to church; another during his grim bivouac in the piney woods, spinning and unspinning his license-plate screws, changing his clothes, a legal criminal: killer, breeder of mice, husband, father. Don't tell me there aren't such men. Don't tell me our great and sovereign state is empty of such men.

He didn't wear a hood. He *owned* a hood, it's true, but no one insisted that he wear it. Hood ownership was ceremonial; the hood was passed down to the next executioner when its previous bearer retired. A symbol of office. Not that Schaumann's superiors would have begrudged him its use. They were traditionalists. The hood was, however, left at home. Even when Schaumann would have preferred to walk hooded to the Chair. It lived in his bureau, the hood. I mean in his armoire. I mean in his dresser. It was folded in with his underwear, the hood. Schaumann's wife knew it was there: she had folded it, as she had the underwear amid or amidst which it resided. She knew about Schaumann's job, though he was, as a rule, taciturn. She probably knew about the mice too. In her basement. It may in fact be a simpler matter to keep one's employment as state executioner secret than to bring mice secretly into one's unadorned home. Especially with two children. The squeaking, the rattling of those filament-thin cage bars, the little corpses, the smell. Why keep secrets in any case? It would not have occurred to Schaumann that a deceit was worth the making. (It would not have occurred to Schaumann that a painting or poem was worth the making.) He covered his tracks without covering his coverings. He covered his tracks with water, not with leaves. And though Schaumann's wife didn't know it, it's no secret that I stole her husband's name from a novel I'm fond of. I'm sure she wouldn't have minded, had she known, so long as she didn't have to read the novel. Her name, however, is still open to conjecture. I go back and forth on this question. What is gained, or not, by naming. In deference to Schaumann, I too am trying to adopt a style of meticulous plainness.

He bred mice in his spare time, in his basement, which was spare. And which, though underfurnished, was decorated like a ship's wheelhouse. I'm serious. It even had a working wheel. Working, in that it spun. More squeaking. Imagine that. Installed before a painted landscape, continuous on every wall. And though he never bothered looking at them, Schaumann's square, flat seas were calm and Mediterranean. A working guardrail was set into the plaster. Working in that one could grip it. Imagine that. All of this was a holdover from the previous owner, who must have had good reasons to spend his money in this way, Schaumann assumed. No one would have accused Schaumann of being capable of such eccentricity. But, then, his character likewise forbade spending his own money, or making a spectacle of his home in order to have such eccentricity removed. And before you get any crazy ideas, neither was it in Schaumann's character to stand on his deck and pick out some figure in the indifferently daubed middle distance, this figure blobbed with what one might suppose, in a charitable moment, was meant to be a muslin frock or robe by whichever rural housepainter had been commissioned to produce this panoramic travesty; Schaumann would never wring some fluffy aesthetic satisfaction out of the figure's artless art, would never wonder about that tanned splotch, never think profound things indicative of his own artless conception of himself as a man, a killer, a breeder of mice, a husband or father, with regard to the figure's static solitude, forever posed observing the motionless ship of his basement not drifting by. He would never feel anything for or about this forgotten digit in a bad painting on the walls of a room about six feet underground on the unexceptional side of the world. No, believe me, none of that for Schaumann. He hardly even—hardly ever—noticed his cubic sea, its two-stroke gulls, its labored clouds, its peeling Etna. He was, as far as representation, like a cat, our Schaumann. Flat birds, you know, squawk not. Painted seas smell only of mildew and plaster. I don't mean Schaumann was unimaginative: mainly uninvested. Mimesis, even when accomplished, even when photoreal, was lost on him. Schaumann went down to his basement not to brood but to breed.

And, while we're setting out some rules, neither did Schaumann see any correlation between his playing vengeful god with his prisoners at the death house and playing fertility god with his mice in their cages. Because Schaumann didn't feel the least bit *empowered*—a word he wouldn't have used, or probably known—by his quotidian killings or propagations. Nor, before you jump to conclusions, was he numb to the unappetizing nature of his work, an unthinking processor of the condemned. It was like this: Schaumann had assistants who helped with the cleanup, and their chatter annoyed him. They had been selected for their solemnity, and yet, "behind the scenes," they talked and talked. They had not been raised right. Schaumann had to assume, therefore, that their fellow guards, all his younger colleagues, assigned to the general prison population, talked even more than they. The others had *lacked* even the solemnity of these chatterers. Sobering to Schaumann. He considered himself lucky, then, to have been plucked from normal duty to work here in the sanctum back in the days when, out there, men who were, like himself, unforthcoming, were still in the ascendancy. He had found such men congenial company. Together unconversing. Strength in silence. Days bygone, or perhaps vanished, or perhaps present but misty in Schaumann's middle distance as he came back from the cafeteria, his awkward shuffle the only movement there in the center of the center, the inside of the inside, where they keep the real if cheerless secrets of Sing Sing. Oh, I don't know: the panopticon, the spirit jars, the fetish bracelets, the guillotine; the different sizes of death chair, with or without cushioned armrests, pillows, claw feet, intaglio images of Itztli, the Ghede, Yama; the shrine to the Rosenbergs, piled with skulls and bowls of rice and mustard greens: the scent of the couple's smolder reproduced by costly parfumeurs and pumped continually into the corridor by unpaid interns. All of which Schaumann passed without remark, breathing symphonically through his one unclogged nostril, carrying his timecard, wondering how many pups from the latest litter aboard his basement might survive till summer.

Would Schaumann's two popinjays have been considered apprentices? Did they nurse hopes of succeeding him and being handed the hood in turn?

But Schaumann insisted on doing all the paperwork

himself. His work signature distinct from his home signature. Left leaning or right, more or less legible, more or less ambitious stroke structures. Hiking each of these mountain ranges in aid of the same Germanic name. Schaumann only wanted to divert attention elsewhere, not dissemble. If someone had asked him what he did for a living, a stranger, though he rarely met any that weren't dead an hour later, Schaumann would have been evasive, but he wouldn't have lied. If cornered. And if you kept at him.

So is it awful? Are they violent?

I'm never alone with them, usually they don't have much fight left by the time I see them.

Are they scared of you?

Not me, exactly.

So exactly what?

He never wrote his memoirs. All his predecessors did. But he had missed killing the Rosenbergs. By just a few years. Can you imagine the sense of professional loss? Schaumann was, at best, occupying the iron age of executioners. The heroes and immortals of the discipline were no more. Really, his profession was itself in danger of extinction. Not the practice but the profession. Courts-martial and the like, they don't require special executioners. It wouldn't be long before Schaumanns were obsolete. So what did he have to brag about? His figure?

I can tell you he was never unfaithful to his wife. Who, in the end, was named Tina, short for Kristina. But Schaumann wasn't much fun to be around. Isn't that also a sort of bad faith? He tried his best with his family; that was obvious; I mean he labored obviously to do his best. It was important to him that people should recognize that he was doing his best. When a poet, or was it a painter, with connections to the so-called New York School opened a small bistro in Schaumann's town, Schaumann wanted everyone to see him take his wife there for dinner. They walked down Main Street and lingered where there might be witnesses. The owner of the restaurant spoke to Mr. and Mrs. Schaumann of a region in Italy where the natives cooked using unwashed basil. They refused to wash it, these aboriginal Italians. They'd pick the leaves and then brush them with twigs. That's all. And so into the sauce. "Such is their reverence for the leaf," said the owner. "Holy God," (cap'd, direct address) thought Schaumann, or perhaps he muttered it. If Schaumann did "have a book in him" after all, it would be the sort of book where people don't *say* but *mutter* (if not *murmur*). I hope that doesn't sound condescending. I don't mean to be, neither toward Schaumann nor the poet turned restaurateur. So don't you look at me that way.

What was it that poet, (or was
he a painter?) just back from
Italy muttered or murmured about
revering his basil?
"Reverence is a twig, water
somehow too familiar.
So don't you look at me that way."

Schaumann bred mice in his spare time, I am told. He was good at it. He experimented, tried to produce litters of only one color, bearing a certain pattern of spots, possessed of a particular nose or eye width. Which is to say that he found mice malleable, as a medium. In time taking special orders from labs from around the state. A little money on the side. Promptly reinvested in his mice. Cages expanding to sheds, additions, new buildings, a veritable farm. And after Schaumann's death, his legacy: glow-in-the-dark mice, monster mice, mice even Schaumann's skilled hands could not have produced: mutated mice, mice of the future. Do you know what a knockout mouse is? It's a mouse whose DNA has been altered to remove or disable a specific gene. For example, the FOXP2 gene, mutations of which supposedly affect language or vocalization. And yes, Schaumann killed many of his failures, whether out of shame or simply to protect his sovereign gene pool. He bought his son or daughter a snake so as to better dispose of the evidence, as he had no assistants attending him in these off-duty executions. But he didn't brag about his mice either, though they were his great success in life: not even in a murmur, not even to the lanky galoot from the city, who would have listened, who would have been eager to take in such nourishing specificity, but who Schaumann recognized as a threat to his (Schaumann's) anonymity. This epicene, glasses-wearing transplant. Wanting to fit in, like Schaumann, but unlike Schaumann talking too much and too strangely to be anything but an anomaly here. Even when using simple words, our urbanite couldn't use them right. And I'm not saying he preferred words that weren't simple. I'm not saying he was *an intellectual*. But he was from a different milieu, that's indisputable. He'd traveled. He'd eaten gritty basil somewhere on a different continent. He'd published poetry in magazines Schaumann wouldn't have heard of, and/or exhibited at galleries Schaumann wouldn't have considered worth a visit. Schaumann would have said, had he been forced to acknowledge such products, "You don't need talent to do what that guy does." But, you know, he didn't consider himself talented, the restaurateur. If you'd asked him at a cocktail party, both of you attending out of obligation, whether he considered himself a talented man, he would have said that his only genius was in being able to locate the word "orgasm" on even the most tightly kerned page of type, almost before his forebrain had taken in ink, page, paper grain; before his mind from its filing cabinets had selected "read" as the verb, "book" the noun, "toadstool" the odor at hand. To which boast you would reply with amusement or embarrassment, wondering whether the trains were still running. Or I guess you'd know best how you would reply.

In fact, when I use the noun *man* to speak about this alien presence in Schaumann's small-town redoubt, it may seem as though I am employing precisely the same noun I would use to speak about our plainspoken executioner, had I likewise deferred giving Schaumann a name. And yet, with regard to the poet-chef, the word *man* in fact has an idiomatic meaning that I'm not sure I can communicate to you—you who are not from around here. But this person, so to speak, would in any case have found Schaumann captivating, had he (the chef) been privy to the things Schaumann would not share. He would have looked at Schaumann as a case study, perhaps to the point of offending Schaumann with his stare; perhaps he would have thought—reviewing Schaumann's future, which was printed in Palatino on the reticent man's cheeks and chin—that the details of Schaumann's life might make a great poem, or painting, or meal. Perhaps *questo grande fabbro* would even have suggested that Schaumann was something of an artist himself, which *is*, probably, condescending; I mean, placing an otherwise indigestible personage into a comfortable context the better to dismiss him. You know how it goes. But, in the chef's defense—let us call him Quakatz, to cut down on the pronouns—Jules Gaspard Ulric Niven van den Quakatz, if you must know—in Chef Quakatz's defense, Schaumann did *produce*, did have an audience. It's just that Schaumann's readers, so called, and critics too, were unable to submit their reviews to the prison board the following morning, for the simple reason (you're way ahead of me) that they were by that time on slabs, smelling of fuse box. What a painting or omelet Quakatz could have made out of that!

Schaumann's mice liked him at least as much as his prisoners did. At least the ones resigned enough to their forthcoming departures to take a moment to appreciate their dispatcher's decorum, his benevolence, his dignity, his melancholy as he led them on his two sinister feet to the long-suffering hot seat; why, some of these hard men even felt sorry for Schaumann. Everyone in the execution party, walking down that long hallway (I am employing my extensive knowledge of cliché), must have felt sorry for one another. For one another, I stress, not for themselves. Schaumann and self-pity didn't mix: he consumed it and excreted it. Like an algae-eating fish cleaning its tank. He consumed and converted into compassion all the self-pity the condemned could not help but produce as they saw their last of this glorious world: the drywall, the drop ceilings, the orangeade light in tubes, the flocculent spiral of discoloration on the tiling by the killing chair itself: Gosh it's hard to leave all this behind! Schaumann knew how to give his charges a proper sendoff. And then the bloody remains in a handkerchief into the trash. Until he went out to the pet store in the next town and bought that snake for his son, anyway. (Do you mind my not looking up the species?) The snake as an intermediary was cleaner, Schaumann thought, than just putting the corpses directly into the bin; the opossum problem was solved just about overnight: no more overturned garbage cans. Offal is offal, yes, whole or first abstracted by snake intestine, but no local, carrion-loving mammal would dare come near the smell of carnivorous reptile.

Sorry, did I say that Schaumann didn't equate his mice and his prisoners? But you know I can't be trusted. I come from a broken home.

The cages, the habitats, the mouse scent filled the Good Ship Schaumann, which despite his supposed disinterest he would have been embarrassed to show Quakatz—Quakatz the tangle, Quakatz the mélange!—and only with great diffidence his wife Tina and his two children, who went unnamed most of their lives. And polishing the fittings on the electric chair, oiling its great big knife switch (don't tell me there wasn't a great big knife switch), Schaumann thought about what sort of creature the union of reptilian Quakatz with his Tina might have produced. What sort of son or daughter would have resulted. What crimes would it commit. How long before it landed before Schaumann the executioner and recognized this man who could have been its sire, but would instead escort it from this welter of sublunary dissatisfactions—oh, matinee stubs, record-club circulars, septic fingers, amber ashtrays, dust-mops and corkscrews and orgasms. An executioner predisposed by his own two parents to attaining a high level of expertise in the arts both of dispatching murderers and husbanding rodents.

Females can become pregnant within twenty-four hours of giving birth, and female pups within five to eight weeks after being born. Schaumann purchased; he culled; he coddled his mice. His human daughter and human son, uncoddled, unresponsive, themselves achieved sexual maturity and took great pains to demonstrate their achievement to their coevals. But they weren't developed enough characters to move away from this burlesque. They went to school locally, they bred with local stock and produced variations so slight from the generations that had preceded them that no researcher could have been seduced into mapping their tiny triumphs. Quakatz, for his part, refrained from breeding. Employed a baker and flourished according to his newer, lower, upstate standards. Kept a diary. Fell in love with and then dismissed said baker. No poem came of this loss. Sad loaves, buns, scones undithyrambed. The baker was solaced soon in the arms of the young and already once-divorced Ms. Schaumann—unworthy, perhaps, of his genius with yeast and oven, but no less so than Quakatz's predawn kitchen, now so undistinguished, where even the weevils had once been elegized.

Did time pass? Every night the restaurateur praying to the Pleiades, Schaumann to the forkhead box. An older Quakatz drove to Albany once to take part in demonstrations demanding the abolishment of capital punishment. Taking food right out of his own mouth, had he known. What with Tina and therefore Schaumann and therefore the death-house payroll office being some of his best customers. Tina and Schaumann ate *chez* Quakatz once a week. A useless expense, now that no one bothered to comment that Schaumann was a good husband to so treat his spouse. But Tina insisted. On Friday nights, perhaps. Along with other couples of retirement age, or nearly, they were regulars. Though Schaumann himself would never retire. If he retired, he might be called upon to say what from. So he would continue pulling that switch so long as his arm would behave as habit and the penal code dictated, without flourish or tremor. And I would say Mr. and Mrs. Schaumann's Friday night ritual was intended to hark or hearken back to the early days of their adolescent pair-bond, but Schaumann and Tina had never dated; they were always married, were born old, and their house contained only a basement. Don't weep for the mice: they have it pretty easy. Short lives, little joy, but lives entire.

Are they scared of you? Schaumann's daughter had asked when she'd gotten her one tour of her father's terraria. And he'd answered: Not me exactly. And she told this to the reporters who found her at the beginning of the next century, still living with her baker, having moved not three hundred yards from her childhood home, now almost entirely given over to mouse breeding—fluorescent mice caged near mice who could not even squeak, because of their mangled FOXP2s.

What took you so long? she asked them, when they knocked. Because all the other state executioners had long since been found, interviewed, published, annotated, celebrated. Not Schaumann, who had left so meager a midden to be sifted by scholars. And Mrs. Baker's bemused testimony made the front page of the local paper, if only rating a peculiar paragraph in the Lifestyle section of the city rag, downstate—where women were women and men were idioms—which by the way made mention of the excellent if coarse pesto being served in the tiny but ominous town's bistro. Ancient Quakatz, long a subscriber, cudgeled his old diaries for some mention of Schaumann the state executioner. Had he fed such a man so regularly and never noted his qualities? It seemed Schaumann was buried not ten minutes from where vacationers now enjoyed gourmet meals priced as though it were still a year when the grease-smoke of fried murderers might have served as a chance condiment for their veal chops. Quakatz visited the grave. Communed with the simple stele. Thought of taking up photography.

The funeral? Unostentatious. The son and his snake, the daughter and her baker, Tina and her names, all in attendance. The two death-row assistants wondering how to ask the widow for their hood back. A very small crowd of retired coworkers from the old days, from the prison—not chatting, not chattering, not gossiping, barely speaking. But calling: *Move over, Schaumann. We're coming in after you. Make room.*

From the grave, muffled, an explanation: "I am trying to adopt a style of scrupulous plainness!"

SAD WHITE PEOPLE

Chris and Chris spent their last night together on the futon, under a feather comforter. Their clothing was mixed up at the foot, sexless stuff—jeans, sweaters—hidden under the bunched sheets and blanket. Both of their bodies—ordinarily quite pale, notwithstanding the angry acne-scar pinpricks on Chris's breasts (this *does* happen), Chris's purple "corpse-hands" due to his congenitally poor circulation—bore subtle blushes, unseen, more pink than red, and wholly unconnected with arousal.

Unaroused, they were in love. They had only been separated twice in as many years. The first time had come eleven months previous, when Chris had left Chris to reunite with her last boyfriend—that guy Marc. Marc was creepy. He'd once bought a cat just to prove he could outstare it, then pushed the animal out of his third story window the one and only occasion that it won. Chris's parents (divorced) mobilized the instant Chris ratted her out. Her father hopped a plane from LAX to LaGuardia within an hour of getting the news, and—though the two hadn't spoken for eleven years—Chris's mother was at the gate to meet him. They went together to an office on the Upper West Side to price an ex-marine trained in deprogramming. They also hired a private detective who'd been in the same unit:

a one-handed man who'd dreamed of cutting a record in Nashville before he was wounded. The detective scoured passenger lists, hung around bus depots, became a regular at Chris's favorite clubs, but turned up no information. Eventually it was discovered that the fugitives weren't even on the run: they'd simply holed themselves up in Marc's Park Slope apartment, having sex, listening to the Velvet Underground, and snorting heroin they'd arranged to have delivered via bike messenger (this *does* happen). Both marines arrived to effect a rescue. Chris was threatened with rehab, Marc with jail for a combination of real charges (possession) and paranoid, fictitious ones (kidnapping, rape). To everyone's surprise, Chris acquiesced immediately: she had just needed, she said, a break. The marine was pleased, but Marc cried and threatened to kill himself, then rushed away to throw up in his bathroom. The affair had lasted two weeks.

The second separation was less exhausting. Chris had visited Prague with her older brother ("The only other man in my life," she would say, employing selective memory). Her parents bankrolled the excursion; they'd proved more pliable than ever after Chris had guaranteed that Marc was no longer a going concern. Her brother was moody, overweight. His favorite quotation: "Always tired, always bored, always hurt, always hating." He claimed, on their flight, that his only remaining aspiration, insofar as women were concerned, was to be given the opportunity—just once—to devastate someone before they devastated him. Chris had kissed him on the cheek (he then scratched the area with the straw poking out of his soda cup) and said for the umpteenth time that she would date him in a second if they were strangers. Which was probably true.

Brother and sister spent a month abroad, and when Chris returned home she had brought gifts: matching bright white cotton Kafka T-shirts and four hits of blinding Czech acid, the latter hidden in an empty film-canister. Chris welcomed Chris back with tears in his eyes: he felt more jealous of the time she'd spent with her brother than he ever had during the Marc debacle. This wasn't because Chris had guessed at the odd, probably unseemly chemistry that existed between Chris and her brother. (Even if he had, the idea of Chris sleeping with other men didn't really bother him.) It was more that he was afraid some intimacy he had never been privy to—a certain memory, laugh, head-tilt, or coital lip-twitch—might be displayed to another person before he'd gotten to see it first. In that arena, how could he compete with a brother, who'd known Chris all her life? This was why Chris was always trying to surprise her, in conversation or bed, with non-sequiturs or grotesque mugging, always hoping to shock her face into some new configuration before somebody else did it for him.

"A face has only so many expressions in its repertoire," he reasoned, "and every given personality only so many responses available to a given stimulus." When Chris started to repeat herself—when Chris's every action brought about a predicted and previously categorized reaction in her—

then he could rest, anxiety free. He would have had the best of her.

"Won't that make me pretty superfluous?" Chris had asked him.

"That's the beauty of it," he said. He would have internalized Chris completely: a model in his memory as complex and complete as the original. He saw this eventuality as the ideal form of their relationship. No matter how far away she was—or who with—they would still, in effect, be together: he the tolerant boyfriend, she the free spirit, roaming and discovering and so forth. No less in love. Togetherness untainted by the least ill will.

As for the acid, he suggested that they drop it that very same night, despite his early class the next morning, despite Chris's grimy jetlag.

"It'll force us to get back in synch," he said.

Chris was game, but this "synch" comment set off alarms. Though her parents approved of Chris, at least in contrast to Marc, her brother did not: he had spent most of their time away insulting him, and his words were still fresh in her mind.

"He has spooky hands," her brother had said. "He has a strangler's hands."

One evening in Prague, when her brother had refused to leave their hostel, Chris had abandoned him for a party of vacationing Laplanders and not returned until the following night. Her guilt regarding this behavior now disposed her to see through her brother's eyes: the scrawny, musteline

Chris seemed a poor exchange for Europe. The way he scrutinized her, as though pricing stock on a jeweler's shelf. She wondered, *What would he do if I weren't around*? Chris had never in her life met anyone else with Chris's odd laissez-faire dependence. It was precisely this quality of his that her brother had attacked. "Where's the sense in dating such a doormat?" he'd asked, as they touched down back in New York. "A doormat with dead man's hands."

The sense, she'd thought, setting her tongue on her bristly upper lip, was that he'd always be there to go home to—even if, under the circumstances, getting there was less than thrilling. She liked that Chris's love for her ticked on all by itself. It was like having a son that you could screw. (We're getting a bit worried about her.) Still, she dropped her army-surplus bags—bearing the faded serial numbers of two dead privates from the one-armed detective's unit—and agreed to take the acid anyway. Maybe it would succeed where she herself had failed, in bolstering her own enthusiasm.

Chris had been the one to introduce Chris to hallucinogens, though that first time it had been mushrooms. This was very early in their relationship, soon after they'd met. Chris had sat in Marc's kitchen eating coffee ice cream, while Chris busied herself around the apartment, waiting for them to kick in. After ten minutes had passed, he asked her, cautiously, "When do the walls start melting?" The mushrooms hadn't been very good—no comparing them to the Prague blotter—and, since taking drugs together had only been a pretense to ease each other into intimacy, Chris and Chris ended up doing what they'd intended to do before the stuff took effect (if it ever did take effect). Chris had therefore linked drugs with fucking. The acid was already working on them when he lifted her sweater over her head and began to suck and bite her nipples. Chris couldn't keep from drumming her fingers lightly on his back. That first time too he had made straight for her chest, worrying at it as though building a nest.

She'd coughed and said, "My breasts—don't really work." (This *absolutely* happens.) An announcement that was the necessary prologue to all of her sexual encounters. Exceedingly tiresome.

Chris looked puzzled. He said, "Well, what does?"

But he hadn't learned his lesson. It remained unlearned after three years, a foible Chris now considered willful ignorance. She humored him this time, as she tended to do, and willed the acid to enter her bloodstream faster.

When it hit, it was devastating. Chris couldn't get it up, then couldn't get his mouth to form the words of his apology. They lay together on the futon, and when, in his body's dry, prickly numbness, Chris located a need to urinate, he found that he was unable to move: he couldn't determine which of their red and white limbs belonged to him. Chris too was lost in their body-tangle, but rather than bemusement, she felt disgust. Her mind returned, over and over again, under an insomniacal compulsion, to the image of her brother—or was it Marc?—berating her furiously for her attachment to Chris. Every word she saw sprayed from those imaginary jowls replaced another measure of her comfort with fear. If she could just work out whose hands were whose, she could make her escape. A black hair on one of their forearms turned like a periscope to regard her.

The next morning, Marc spotted them coming out of a gourmet grocery in Greenpoint. Chris had decided to skip his class so that they could spend an entire day together. Chris was moody and silent, but this was common behavior after a night of "debauchery"; Chris paid it no mind, and chattered on about how little had happened while Chris was abroad. The day was bright and cold. Sunlight came off all the local reflective surfaces, making Chris fix her eyes on the sidewalk.

Seeing them together always gave Marc a pain in his stomach he imagined was similar to the ulcer he planned on having. Wrapping the butt of his hotdog in its paper, he began to trail after the Chrises, taking short breaths of the sharp air through his mouth. When he was near enough to the couple to see the yellow hairs on the back of Chris's neck, he detoured down a cross street to move parallel to them and eventually head them off at the pass.

Chris glanced back at this moment, jaw still aching from the acid, probably being paranoid. She opened her mouth to tell Chris that she thought she had seen Marc, but, before she could, a rectangular sheet of glass, moving horizontally—six feet long and four wide, less than a quarter of an inch thick—whisked off both their heads like crumbs from a vinyl tablecloth.

The glass had been the outermost layer of a many-paned window—fifth from the left on the thirty-second floor of an office building, one block away. Forty years earlier, when a firm of Brooklyn glaziers, long defunct, had installed the window, a certain adhesive had been in use, one later revealed to be water-soluble. The manufacturer sent out warnings and refunds, but the glass-makers never noticed: it was a family business, and the patriarch's eldest had refused to take the reins at a crucial point, preferring to waste his time with his pansy friends till at last, and to everyone's satisfaction, he came down with something fatal and expired in Bellevue weeks before his father managed to track him down. Deprived of new blood, the company—and the family—lost focus, dispersed, depleted; and so, with no one the wiser, the pane, this one alone, out of hundreds of candidates, had gradually lost its hold on its molding, on its building, through generations of rain and snow. Finally it peeled off, top to bottom, and began to drift, feather-smooth, slicing its way to ground.

Singing like a saw under a practiced bow, the glass had pendulum'd in widening arcs, avoiding any obstruction that might have shattered it, projecting a dimple on the faraway pavement when it swung into line with the sun. It was a jubilant flight. Consider: the pane had suffered forty years with a single, fixed view, seen complexions clear and cloud inside the office, ties lengthen and skirts shrink, hairlines recede—countless faces excavated by age. Once, a man in possession of the pane's office for less than a year had hanged himself with his snakeskin belt. He'd burned both hands securing his noose from the small, thick-painted pipe that traveled through the room just below the ceiling, on its way to the bathroom, where a colleague was scraping his shirttail clean of semen under a stream of scalding water. The suicide choked with his hands still stinging, and the pane reflected his expression of plump bewilderment. The corpse's feet swung with great momentum toward the window, bouncing off the thick inner sheet, sending vibrations through the two other layers that would hasten the outermost pane's departure by nearly a decade.

Local pigeons—kept alive through the winter by roosting on windowsills leaking people-heat—saw the pane's descent as meandering, interminable. It looked to them something like a heat-mirage, a traveling wobble of light. If any of the birds' human benefactors had noticed it, they might have seen a streak: a straight gray line or else one curved like a sail by an updraft, that's all. Seen from above the glass might have resembled a playing card: from the right angle a viewer could have caught his or her reflection framed there as its royal (one-eyed, holding a butter knife, perplexed). A tiny spider that had been trapped on the interior, making a cozy living as the traffic of gnats increased with the pane's peeling, didn't notice its flight at all. There was no need to cling for dear life: air washed both sides of the sinking window but didn't even ruffle the burnished bristles on its legs. Life being denser for the spider than it was for the pigeons, the trip lasted what would amount to weeks of relative human time, give or take. The spider was only thrown loose when the pane came to a rest, landing intact and spattered by two red Rorschachs on a sidewalk square chalked with a white and arrowed heart.

Some minutes later, a woman running up the street accidentally set foot on the glass. It shattered with a voluptuous crack, and she slipped among the shards. She didn't recognize them as the remains of a brief but luminous freedom.

THE TERRIBLE RIDDLES OF HUMAN SEXUALITY (SOLVED)

1. Pink and blue rabbits, in pairs, in rows; heads together, sniffing; each body cocked forward, each bunny intrigued; white background and two pink buttons on a side-stitch. *What am I?*

(*Answer:* It's an old superstition that wearing children's panties under the uniform will bring in more trade. May claimed they were for a niece when she bought them. She took the two cellophane packages to a restroom and tried on a pair. It was almost exciting. The tightness, or maybe the rabbits' sincerity.)

2. Balloon sounds, deep indentations in the skin. A sharp, worrisome pain. The smell of plastic, like a booth in a diner. *What am I?*

(*Answer:* May puts on her uniform long before she needs to be at work. She's trying to get herself used to it. Wearing it feels like being scared. No deep breaths, as after running.

The weather is warm, but May can't bring herself to go out in the outfit uncovered. Some of the other girls do. May thinks they look like hookers, coming in to work. Her boots she doesn't mind people seeing. They're steel-toed, which costs extra, but they give the right clunk on stairs and tile. May thinks they look cute, really, below the oversized, rumpled red sweater she wears to keep incognito—and the six or so inches of nyloned thigh that peek out between them and the sweater's thickly stitched hem. May imagines kicking the shit out of the first guy on the street to make fun of her getup. It'd be easy with all that extra weight. At work, though, she has to be careful. High-heeled numbers with pinched and pointy toes are the norm there. Dainty but forbidding. With this extra weight, May has to know her own strength.

To her face the other, older girls call her their little soldier boy. Behind her back it's "Leadfoot.")

3. Yelling from 3E, television from 2W, garlic 2E, music 1W, and no sign of life in 1E, as ever. Keys cold between index and middle, middle and ring, ring and pinky, like claws. *What am I?*

(*Answer:* It takes longer heading out to work than getting back. There's less traffic, of course, at quitting time—the streets are deserted. Every night she thinks, "The streets are deserted." Even the walk upstairs to her apartment seems abridged, coming home.)

4. St. Christopher, Catwoman, Krishna, and Christ. Black and white Catherine Deneuve under a bedsheet. Mardi

Gras beads and a snow globe from Texas—yellow sand, plastic cacti, and a russet armadillo. *What am I?*

(*Answer:* The taxi's dashboard has the contents of a junk drawer glued to it with creamy white Elmer's. The driver is bald, and the back of his head is dotted with liver spots. These don't reflect the light of passing streetlamps. May watches white blobs curve down his pale scalp: disappearing, reappearing.)

5. Large and purple pastries filled with grape, threatening to drip down over a tobacco-stained counter on which loose gray hairs stir in the air conditioning. *What am I?*

(*Answer:* May can imagine the texture of the driver's ears in her mouth. Cartilage is sexier than skin or bone. She is assembling a book of aphorisms. May sees her mouth in the rearview: wide, with perfect square herbivore's teeth. She spots lipstick on an incisor, even in the darkness of the cab, and takes out her hankie to erase it.)

6. A mountain of intricate women, naked, hairless, tarnish-green and bruised: clinging to one another by breast and buttock. Then, adrift in the sky, lovers engaged in a variety of forms of fornication—thirty or so pairs of Paolo and Francesca making an inverted funnel, stained teeth bared, aureoles and fingernails similarly tinted, whirling, a violet tornado. *What am I?*

(*Answer:* Midway up the stairs to work, May's boss Milton has hung two paintings he considers very classy. Clunk clunk clunk.)

7. Baseball game on the radio. Two men, one standing, the other in black silk pajamas on a four-poster with posts bent and splintered at their tops, the ceiling scarred, sooty.

   "Hey May," the pajama-man says. Standing-man leaves, brushing past her. She twists away from the contact. Her ribcage is a shrill whistle in that uniform. "What do you think, is two thousand dollars enough to cut someone's hands off?" pajama-man asks. "I mean, if you got the offer? I mean, how much would make you not think twice?"

   "More than that," May says.

   "By how much?"

   "Considerable."

   What am I?

(*Answer:* Milton's office is the first room you pass, just off the landing. He says he settled there to see the customers coming in, but his door is always closed, and Milton is usually asleep. He should have bedsores by now, the other girls say. They get him to take them down the street for Chinese, or else to inspect their rooms and equipment. That's what the boss is supposed to do. Keep on your feet, Milton—vertical isn't so hard. But Milton says he's tired.)

8. May complains, "I don't think they like me."

"You're being paranoid," Milton says.

"They don't like having me around."

"Tough to be the new girl," Milton says.

"They don't ask me out for drinks. They leave the room when I come in."

"They're busy," Milton says. "Maxine and Mildred have kids."

"They don't trust me."

"They don't know you."

"They stare."

"They're jealous."

"They won't leave me alone with the customers."

"That's customary," Milton says.

"They make me leave my door open. Afraid I'll give customers executive relief. For bigger tips. Lure trade away. Take money out of their pockets."

"Say 'handjob,' May. 'Executive relief' is vulgar."

What am I?

(*Answer:* May imagines men milling around the street outside, raincoats slung over their shoulders. Why don't they come in?)

9. This cloud of tiny black lines and angles. Drifting els, sees, and jays. A soft sticky rain that tickles the face. *What am I?*

(*Answer:* May clobbers a centipede with tissue box. She thinks she feels some of its broken legs land and stick on her forehead, standing vertical, making up a new hairline. The rest get lost in her sweater. There are little itches on her stomach and shoulders now. The bug's body, bald, she retrieves and wraps in a tissue; both go down the toilet. May washes her hands and goes back to checking her makeup in the bathroom mirror. One face. She shakes it back and forth and up and down, trying to dislodge the legs, making her neck pop and crack. Soon there's a cloud of dust or dandruff and sweater-strands that coil and float in front of her. Her scalp starts itching too.)

10. Chains sprouting from swelling red vinyl walls. A divan cushioned in the same material; it whooshes out air when compressed by a body. A flyswatter and a chocolate bar on a short wooden table. *What am I?*

(*Answer:* May waits three hours in the Justine Suite before she gets a customer. Men are drifting in steadily now, but they're the regulars; they get assigned to the senior girls, with whom they have longstanding professional relationships. May makes sure to bring a book to work; she's gone nights with no trade at all. She reads while she waits on the divan. Sometimes the phone rings, startling her: the new girl has to take the calls. She speaks politely to nervous, skeptical men. Occasionally a woman, but they chicken out without fail—she's never known one to show up. The callers ask for directions, sometimes the price-list. May has to answer in whichever persona she's using. Odd days she's Chloe, even she's Mistress Jocasta. Tonight she's Chloe.

Her first customer of the night is middle-aged and clean. He carries a leather briefcase, probably come straight from work. He smells like fenugreek and mouthwash. He's just been briefed, in the foyer, on Milton's standards and practices: no scarring, no sex, nothing illegal. Though Milton suspects—correctly—that the girls themselves are flexible on these points. They don't offer; they wait for their customers to broach the subject. Decisions are made on an individual basis. They still will not gratify in any conventional sense: they are not prostitutes. Most, however, can be convinced to breach certain statutes of the city health code. The penalties for this are negligible compared to a vice rap. Old men pissing in alleys would get the same charge.

May greets her customer. She stretches and stands, a tight-wrapped cylinder, her outfit squeaking. She imagines being slipped into an Edison phonograph and rotated, the needle bearing down and playing her as she spins. She wonders what sort of music she'd let out.)

11. A tube of toothpaste, a toothbrush, a stapler, a jar of mayonnaise, three paper clips, a rubber bone, a pocket fan, a blindfold, three rolls of quarters, pancake mix, a nine-pin, two thousand dollars in cash, a Japanese radish, a water pistol, carpet samples in beige and white, fifty yards of twine, a yellow pad, a phone-book, a foun-

tain pen, a brass alarm clock, a clown's nose, a cowboy hat, fishnet stockings, a bottle of mineral water, a jump-rope, a square foot of Astroturf, a baguette, a nail-file, an inflatable flotation device, rubber gloves, felt gloves, three handkerchiefs, a false beard, a wig (blonde), a wig (white), a football, five refrigerator magnets with painted representations of classical composers, a slender vase, a box of Epsom salts, and a VHS copy of Lucille Ball in *The Fuller Brush Girl* (1950). *What am I*?

(*Answer:* The customer's briefcase is full of strange shapes. May, on tiptoe, can't keep from trying to see the combination he dials to open it. She does not hear his instructions the first time.

He says, "We'll just keep trying until we find something that works."

May, clicking her cuffs shut, asks demurely what this means.)

12. Her age in hours and days and seconds—childhood phone-numbers—the rules of backgammon—nursery rhymes—Oscar Wilde—ways to differentiate male and female butterflies—the distance between the Earth and the Sun in furlongs—the atomic weight of carbon. *What am I?*

(*Answer:* May tries to distract herself as the customer goes about his business. His briefcase is open beside him, at her feet. She is brought back, always brought back to the sight of the top of his head. It's beneath her; she doubles her chin to see it. His hair is thinning at the top, damp and matted from exertion. Poor thing, she thinks.)

13. An unfamiliar woman sitting in a cold bath. She's listening to Bach. Her back is turned. She is killing herself. Blood moves over the lime that's growing on the tarnished tub, over the side, onto the toilet, everywhere. The tepid water wobbles around her feet, which are wedged by the faucet, making them grow and shrink with the tide. Her toenails begin to look polished. *What am I?*

(*Answer:* In his dream, Milton can't speak. He makes a great effort, needing to tell the woman that she's doing it wrong: the bathwater should be hot. Amateurs are the ruin of every profession. He is assembling a book of aphorisms. He is tortured by his helplessness. When he wakes up, he can't be sure the dream isn't a memory. Who was she? He feels terribly guilty. It takes some time to sort it out.

He likes it when May stops in his office to talk, or just sit around while he sleeps. He sleeps better when there are people keeping him company. His building is old and infested with bugs; he's terrified of them crawling on him while he can't feel it. Which would be worse than feeling it. But they won't come out while there's activity in the room—someone awake, watching the TV, reading a magazine. Just sitting there, for fuck's sake. The girls knock off at three in the morning, and then someone usually peeks in to see how he's doing, hoping to be taken out for a meal. He gives in, usually. When he can work up the energy to eat.)

14. Chromatische Fantasie d-moll, or Fantasie chromatique en ré mineur, or Fantasia cromatica in re minore, if you have a preference. *What am I?*

(*Answer:* A tinny piano piece from Milton's radio concludes just as the customer is withdrawing, leaving money in May's paperback, marking her place. It's ten minutes before one of the other girls looks in, made suspicious by the quiet, ready to quash any violation of house-etiquette. She unchains May and takes her to the bathroom. May brings along her book. She washes her one face and counts her money.

"That's some boodle," May's coworker says—or that's the gist of it—indicating the tip. "What did he want—did he want the old golden showers?"

"No," says May.

"No, that's too pedestrian. He wanted cutting, then? Little slices off his butt? He brought a bunch of pins from new shirts, which he's been saving in a cardboard earring box? Pearl-headed?"

"Not at all," says May.

"Racist stuff? Call him kike and whatnot? Put your storm-trooper boots into the small of his back?"

"I'm Chloe," says May. She sits on the lid of the toilet. "I didn't do anything to him. Jocasta does the doing."

May puts her book down on the gummy floor, her chest and lower back tingling. There's a pain in the right side of her body, as though someone had yanked it foot-first out of alignment with her left. Still bent, she holds her ankles, massaging them.

"Well," May's coworker says, a little concerned, "what did *he* do to *you*?")

15. Landscapes of sand or prickly evergreen leaves; shoji screens; cold lodestone mountains; old iron walkways; hot asphalt avenues; mesa shelves and tundra. *What am I?*

(*Answer:* May cannot fathom herself. She feels phantom foreign objects of various textures on and inside her body.

"It was a circus," she says. She will not say more. She longs to get back into a cab, to curl onto its seat. But it's hours yet until she's off. And then she'll still need to see Milton.)

16. "You ever have a sweetheart?" one of the other girls is asking. They like to tease; they want to know more about him—how did he get into the business, and who took care of him before they came around? Milton kicks his blanket and sheet into eddies around his legs.

    "Not so's you'd notice."

    "It'd be easier on you if you went out sometimes," says the girl.

"You'd think so," says Milton. May sits by the radio, tuning. She finds a violin.

"So what's the problem?" asks the girl.

Milton is getting dressed. He has Velcro straps on his shoes, a clip-on bow tie. "I couldn't be bothered," he says. "I never really wanted it."

To May, his interrogator says, "Isn't it funny that men can only manage it when they want to."

May remembers a few bars from the middle of the piece. She was wide open when she heard it, and tunes catch so easily in her head. Many of the regular customers insist on their girls bringing music to work by. May wonders what could possibly be appropriate to the job. Until today, nothing she could think of would have fit. Nothing would *work* with the work. You could try to make it pretty, but what could make it pretty? You could try and make it uglier, but how to find sounds less appealing than the balloon-animal squeaks natural to the business? The best thing would be to find something to make the work feel necessary. The best thing would be to find something to make the work seem essential.

"We do essential work," says May, sifting through the static.

What am I?

(*Answer*: They adjourn to Hunan Palace.)

THE DANDY'S GARROTE*

From the moment I picked your book up until the moment I laid it down, I was sitting on my sofa at the time, you probably remember, I mean the green one, it was hot and rainy, I looked at the words and letters, I understood then what it meant for the marks on a page to "swim" in front of one's eyes, it was quite a trick, they swam in my eyes in the heat and I worked to turn every page, such a labor it was, but I owe you that much, don't we read one another out of a sense of *debt*, aren't you sweating on your own green sofa waiting for me to find myself robbed of agency and motive power and every sense save smell by the brilliance of your latest book and then nonetheless to stand and walk the streets and deliver to your doorstep my encomium in fifty to a hundred words; but even with this swimming and this labor and the heat and the thunder and the damp tapping on the wide-leafed plants out my window that give me such a rash when I brush past them, I could see that you had finished me, I mean really done for me, that you'd eaten me entire, I could wait for the end of the storm and the end of the heat but what else was there to wait for, my

**Editor's note:* The author was asked to provide a blurb for the debut novel of an old and dear friend. He delivered the above text. It was returned.

future was already in the swim on your pages, you've stolen everything I was waiting to learn might still belong to me, so what point in reading, what point in closing my windows so the wet won't warp the pages in the library made irrelevant by the addition of your opus, I was there on the page already, I was already curling in humility on my green sofa in your novel; from that moment I mean until the moment when robbed of agency and motive power and every sense save smell I knew I had to stand nonetheless and walk the streets empty outside of a dog here and there to find your home and ascend your steps and smile at your neighbors speaking Spanish under a republic of six bewildering wind chimes to deliver my most sincere endorsement, much as anticipated in your book, where I stand atremble, using words like "atremble," my hand on your buzzer or doorknocker, anticipating your reaction, your expression, as I concentrate and condense and massage my honest admiration into a few simple phrases and tell you how your book—good Christ, your book—taxes the vocabulary of *watch your fucking back.*

II.

She has you on board the very next morning, and you are old enough to know that something is different, that something has happened which must matter a good deal. Your mother doesn't notice your confusion. She is lively and excited.

"The twins play those games all the time," she says of you, "dressing in each other's clothes—adorable. They can read head to head on our settee, one upside-down one right side up. We could show you later on, if you'd come to our stateroom. Or they could do it for you now?"

She's all too happy to speak with the older man who's contrived to come and join you in the short time since castoff. She's no longer the person you knew ashore, the hysteric who would lock herself in the broom-closet to write letters to God when she'd been contradicted. (I know one of you has a page of her latest epistle shut in a new French grammar. You found the paper in my wicker wastebasket, and a finger of the basket's straw picked at your sleeve when you stole it. It's marred by a crab-shaped ink stain, and begins *Tell me, Sir, whether I may ask you for another favor.*) Aboard the steamer she's back in her element, the urbane traveler, and you children—Willie, Nillie—are only her accessories, matching luggage. This doesn't embarrass or upset you (as it will when you're older); hearing your collective talents enumerated you can't help but grin, lopping the opposite sides of your two smiles like facing panels of a dressing mirror.

The man, Mahaffy, who resembles our family doctor, knocked off his own hat to chase it to your mother's side; he bent down to retrieve it and then asked for her arm to help him upright: a little vaudeville, executed with confidence. He's sizing you up. He says, approvingly, "Scamps. Rascals. Scalawags and scapegraces." The ship is lousy with old men. En route for a last look at Paris. You both shake hands with Mahaffy. Above, four black and red stogies fumigate the sky. There is cheering, the foghorn, and your mother's pleasant alto as she small-talks with this stranger. The bitterness of her cigarillo (he'll have offered; she won't know how to refuse), her velvet glove-hairs whispering under your nails, your dockside sarsaparillas turning sour on your tongue.

There are also men closer my age, off to cure their shell-shock with a second dose of Europe. Your mother, bless her, doesn't care for the shabby way they dress, their smooth, pale faces or lacquered hair; how they're frightened to show their wallets when they have to tip a porter. Seeing them at the guardrail, morose, getting tight, she'll think of how she used to tease that I'd gotten her pregnant just to stay out of the war. She says, "I'm marrying my schoolyard sweetheart if you please. My boys'll have a Parisian childhood. New York and their atherfay just memories." But she has ten sealed envelopes in her purse, addressed Dearest William and Dearest Nathanael, one for each day of your trip. They took three days to write, copy, and seal. (I barely had three days' notice.) She's keeping them safe, keeping to our agreement: one letter for each night at sea.

You kids wonder whether this schoolyard beau of hers exists, or if he's just another imaginary correspondent. Furry, overstuffed Mahaffy—a Volsteadist—is scandalized by this talk of divorce. He offers another cigarette to avoid responding as his conscience dictates. Your mother declines, more comfortable now, and says, "The best thing for them. The best thing in the world."

Mahaffy thinks of his own youth. He had just the sort of childhood your mother is imagining, *la vie de chateau*, and is now on what he reckons will be his final pilgrimage. He looks you boys over as you continue to do your mirror-routine, and wonders if the affliction he suffers—this need to roll himself, little piggy, in the smells and colors of his own French adolescence—will affect you, seventy years down the line, as irresistibly as it has him. He pictures identical octogenarians on some future ship: an ornithopter with feathered oars beating the air.

"Bravo," says he. "Continental education. In what trade did you say your former husband ah?"

And you children answer, proudly, Architect, as your mother wraps three pink fingers around the outsize beads she's strung on her wrist. She calls me a layabout, which is the sort of word one only sees in novels; she doesn't mention the one building to my credit, though even there, from the ship, you can see it vibrating like a long, taut thread on the horizon. (I can also see it here, from my office window. There are lights on in one of the upper stories: other work that lasts the night.) And what possibilities an architect-father should pose! At his drawing board, drafting three-tiered underground fairy-barrows, inverted baroque palaces, with stables for ants and rats and sparrows, and courtyard guillotines that work backwards—the blades *rising* through the neck—hoisted with spider-silk cables up a wedge-thin shaft by birds fleeing spears at their backsides . . .

And, in your memories, this ideal father, the one who built you cloud-castles, eclipses me, who never did. You have an urge to spring to his defense, but a clandestine elbow-tap from Willie to Nillie ensures your remaining conspiratorially silent.

"Many's the fortune started from no legacy," says the old man, also an architect's son.

"They'll be well set up," your mother answers, wondering if this is so. She imagines her fiancée collecting her at Rouen; the boys plopped into the back seat of his car with a wizened aunt or mother.

Mahaffy coughs and makes a show of patting his pockets for his cigarette lighter. It's the kind meant for use in the parlor or car, the size of a small soda siphon; he carries it for its exceptional longevity. He hides his second cigarillo of the evening in his beard, and presses both thumbs on the trigger, singeing his gray whiskers and the black brim of his topper. You fear for a moment that his thick fur coat will ignite—maybe catching your mother's wrap and the sailor's caps she's bought you—but are reassured by the presence of so much water. Fires onboard must be met, you think, with good humor and insouciance. You imagine the captain, Mahaffy's double, sitting at table in a white and black uniform, both hands on his punchbowl belly, watching your mother knock over a candlestick as she reaches for the jam; he gives a jovial chuckle and bids her be calm as his long, smooth table burns, licking the papered ceiling. "Never mind," he says, basso profundo like his foghorn. "We'll just open a window."

But the captain is really a young, thin fellow of the sort your mother affects to disdain. An ex-Navy man, mustered out as a lieutenant junior, he is nervous at the beginning of this, his first voyage in command. Like his father, who procured him this position, and, for that matter, the old man talking to your mother, he is a member of the Anti-Saloon League. The captain is terrified of the moment when his vessel—a Cunard liner, out of England—will enter international waters. He is convinced that the passengers will glut themselves on the store of spirits in the hold, thereby leading to an orgy of misrule for which alone he will be responsible. In his civvies—against regulation during departure—he leans on the guardrail, passionately drinking quinine water. He composes a letter to his father while he waits to be discovered. *Even though*, it will begin, *I quake with trepidation and sickness of heart, I must write to request a release from the duties you have so graciously*

“Nothing wrong with wealth well earned,” Mahaffy is saying, thinking of his inheritance, also of the money he’s willed against his lawyer’s wishes to an illegitimate son in San Francisco.

It’s the first mate, a fifty-six year old veteran of the Spanish-American War, who is seeing the liner underway—up in the wheelhouse, in full company regalia. He was discharged as a major; the rank still precedes his name on his pension checks. Some of the younger porters address him in this fashion, frightened for their jobs.

When tourism was down, during the war, he had found temporary employment as a traveling Four Minute Man delivering propaganda speeches for the Committee on Public Information as the reels were changed in motion-picture houses. In the office, and earlier in Cuba, he had witnessed great things: moments of history. The Rough Riders had been aboard one the ships he served on, and he himself had enjoyed a short discussion about trade unions with Roosevelt. At a CPI office to gather notes for his next round of speeches, he had been present when the decision was made to rechristen sauerkraut “liberty cabbage.” He fantasizes about corkscrewing holes in the hull. Though it’s unlikely he could ever sink the liner by this method, he likes picturing—while he gives listless and irresponsible orders to the helmsman—his choirboy captain brought low by a barroom appurtenance. He has drafts of the report already written, hidden in his cabin safe: *Never before in my years of service have I witnessed so flagrant a disregard*

"He's a prince," your mother says, speaking of my replacement. "An honest-Injun prince." She's determined to humble Mahaffy. Mahaffy, to his credit, is onto her. This lady has something to prove. She'll hound him the entire trip—each meeting an opportunity to embellish her anticipated affluence.

"He isn't French by birth. He's Bengali," she adds. "He has royal blood. His family doesn't approve of me."

And these lies lead me into a kind of sympathy with your mother. We neither of us can be sure you'll approve of the trips we construct for you—hers real, if hyperbolized, and mine wholly counterfeit: this attempt, too late, to build your fairy kingdom with words. How mundane it is when set beside the pictures I imagine you imagine that I might have made to entertain you. I remember what *I* loved as a child: smut, sugar, cruelty, and Ambrose Bierce. Must I assume that you, as my sons, share these feral predilections? (It was his story "One of Twins," itself in the epistolary mode, that first came to my mind when you were born—in which a surviving twin takes revenge on the man responsible for his brother's death. I remember that the antagonist regards the twin with a *look of unspeakable terror*, for *he thought himself eye to eye with a ghost.*) I'd rather believe that your similarity protects you, that your thoughts are a system closed to the wicked world: a private language, your uterine Morse, keeping the rest of us out. But I can't run the risk of being too tame for your tastes. Our relationship has been reduced to this: whether or not I can keep you reading.

"Tommyrot," Mahaffy says to your mother. "Moonshine. They're savages not to approve of a pretty thing like you."

"His parents," your mother replies, "did not have the benefit of a Continental education."

On the rail, the captain sniffs. There is an odor in the air that provokes a terrifying memory. His father, naked. Drinking brandy in the garden. Red genitals, upturned face. Or is he thinking of Noah? There is the unmistakable scent of alcohol underneath the bracing bay-smell.

A porter, just five years your elder, arrives now to tug impertinently at your mother's hem. He says, "Your state-room's ready, ma'am." He says, "It's *been* ready." But she can't be bothered. She's found her audience.

"Why don't you boys go down and explore?" she suggests. "Then you can come back and show me the way, give me the nickel tour." She doesn't look at you. The more she talks to the old man, the more firmly she believes in her new future. She doesn't notice the gentleman's disappointment at your having been removed. The porter, in turn, regards you with suspicion—as though your twinness is a trick intended to secure his favor. At thirteen, he's the youngest employee on the ship. You're the only ones onboard over whom he can assert some sort of authority.

"C'mon," is what he says. He jerks his thumb over his shoulder then turns on his heel. Inside into the warmth, and down the wide flight of stairs. There is a constant, tooth-tickling vibration. You smell wax and brine and burgundy wine. The porter hopscotches along the pattern of alternating red diamonds on the vestibule's carpeting until he reaches a second descending flight; he looks back to see if you've followed his lead, determined to turn this little trek into a drill. You hop obediently to his side, in the process passing a dimly lit ballroom. Three couples and a woman alone have begun a slow-drag two-step to the accompaniment of the motor. Empty bottles oscillate at their feet. In her hand, the lone woman holds a page of creased onionskin. This is a message from her fiancé, who is still stationed in Germany, apologizing for having married a young Frenchwoman in her stead. He met the girl while in hospital for three puncture wounds to the shoulder. The letter is signed *Ever Regretful.* Having already purchased her ticket, the woman decided to take the trip regardless. It will be her first time out of the country. You and she pass in opposite directions, on either side of the open double doors.

Deeper into the ship—hallways lit with bulbs fixtured in shell shapes—your porter spies the Major. The boy loses his swagger. For the past half hour he has been leading you in circles; has in fact led you past your stateroom five or six times, counting on the sameness of the corridors to keep you disoriented. If he were to be questioned, he would have to admit to this misdemeanor. But something is wrong—the Major is smiling. He's soaking wet, and hiding something in his left hand. He actually pats the porter on his head as he walks by—doesn't box his ears for slouching. This breach of protocol makes the porter uneasy. He takes you directly to your room now, closing the door behind you and locking you in with his master key. It makes him feel better.

The porter winds his way back toward the deck to assist the next party. He grew up without a father, just as you'll have to do; not because his father was awkward or unsure around children—their little inscrutable faces—and not because the porter's mother deprived the boy of his company, but because no one was sure who his father was. *Two weeks*, the porter will write later that evening, *and that bum had better be out of the house.* He'll send the letter back with his wages from port, to impress his mother's neighbors with the French stamp and postmark. Maybe he won't wait: the eldest of his five cabin-mates has a book of pretty stamps from all over the world. He bought it, he said, at a store that sold Turkish cigarettes and dirty playing cards; the stamps were the cheapest thing on offer. Happily, some of the stamps have girls on them too—holding lamps or shields, and often with a breast exposed. Another stamp shows a hussar on the back of a rearing roan, foam mapping the animal's grimace. The hussar brandishes a curved sword, but has turned his face to the right, looking with surprise at something beyond the perforated border of his landscape. Is this unseen element what's caused his horse to rear? The sky is red behind them, and there is a walled city visible in the middle distance. This man, the porter reckons, though perhaps not pictured at his best, would issue forceful, authoritative missives to his generals, and sign them with his seal in runny wax: *Tonight we charge when the first star shines.* He hopes his letter to his mother will have a similar tone. He knows he was lucky to get this job. He has learned to protect himself—for who else could do it?—by always being on the attack.

Trapped in the cabin, you wonder what's happening on deck. You imagine the porter coming back into the air, and Mahaffy noting the boy's broad, Cro-Magnon cranial structure. Your mother is a beauty, as you well know, but she had been characteristically narcissistic in her assumption that the old man was staging the routine with his hat in order to proposition *her*. It was you, Willie and Nillie—you're suddenly quite sure—that caught his interest. Mahaffy, that other architect's son, was once a doctor. Not a medical doctor, you tell one another, but a seller of patent medicines by mail. Gullible women—like your mother—would write him and beg him to cure their children of monstrous deformities or fatal illnesses. And he would respond, unfailingly, that *Even my poor heart, Madam, hardened like Pharaoh's before the libels of Moses by the witness of so much human suffering, could not help but be moved by your words of gracious Mother's Love and Concern.* Probably he has long been on the run from the Health Department, and carries a large bounty on his head. Unknown to the authorities (you warm to your story) he is also responsible for the deaths of twenty-five children of both sexes, ranging in age from five to fourteen. These were not due to his inaccurate diagnoses (though he had once, by virtue of his ignorance, you giggle, depopulated an entire family farm in Darkest Maine) but to an avocation he had acquired only peripheral to his stated profession. The old man, having no aptitude for modern medicine, had become fascinated with obsolete, often arcane procedures. His favorite of these to perform, inspired perhaps by that song "The Tutankhamen Rag," of which you're both so fond, was the removal of the brain through the nasal cavity with long, curved hooks. Your identical physiognomies, it's only natural, and the grace of your synchronized movements, he found enthralling. The hooks, and other items from his collection—some made-to-order, others honest-Injun antiques—are in the false center of his large burgundy portmanteau. He wants time alone with you both, to examine your skulls; perhaps to see how the one's organs differ, if at all, from the other's. Afterward he could preserve what he had removed in small, prepared metal amphorae; or, if he wanted to be true to his predecessors, simply discard them.

Each time he performs the procedure, or the score of others he's mastered (as he never could the simple suture, the subcutaneous injection), he is troubled by this very decision, you decide. How true to his forebears should he remain? He's felt the occasional twinge of guilt, appropriating those wonderful, ancient, misguided rites for his own gratification—and on those occasions would do everything in his power to execute them accurately. Other times, however, he's told himself that it didn't matter—was it not their very irrationality that made the procedures so captivating? Why not improve or simplify them, then, when time or hygiene became issues? In this your Mahaffy resembles the composers of the "Tutankhamen Rag" that encouraged him (or, for that matter, the "Shakespearean," "San Juan," "Halley's," or "Hophead"): clothing venal preference with history. The comparison would never occur to Mahaffy, however—nor to you. This Mahaffy feels that he's been establishing a legitimate connection to his heritage—the continuing saga of quackdom—while you, Willie and Nillie, pass the time telling macabre stories about old men who like to kill children. Up on deck, your mother puts the finishing touches on her fantastic luck. And I, in my office, have become ashamed of my arrogance. I don't know a thing about any of you. I don't know a thing about the world. And yet there is no way for the world to correct me. And if you, any of you, were here, I wouldn't be interested in a thing you had to say.

Mahaffy is distracted now by a splash and cries of "Man overboard!" In your stateroom you turn to see the captain drop past a porthole. Standing on chairs to look down at the waterline you watch him thumped against the hull. Certain his head was powdered by the fall, he feels salt swish around his skull—seeing water and swallowing it. Stubborn, he surfaces, and at my desk I wonder whether your mother will keep her promise after all and give you my letters. In the street, later tonight, at the feet of four or five high-rises—and mine a few blocks down and over—I'll note for the umpteenth time that it's impossible to tell that I'm walking on an island; that, a few miles away, the buildings float. Later still, Mahaffy will be embarrassed to hear the ship's doctor diagnose the captain with cinchonism—known to cause dizziness and a ringing in the ears, brought on by an excess of quinine. (*Request first mate take command*, a telegraph to the head office will read, *but unable to locate.*) Embarrassed, that is, because he himself would have guessed melancholia. The vapors. Or else delirium tremens. He promises himself that he will offer the poor fellow some of his patented (if, strictly speaking, illegal) magnetic anti-bilious tablets. Did you, looking out through the double-paned glass, hope that he would drown?

Two stars are visible in the sky, ringed round with knotted cloud. Your mother has stopped speaking. Inspiration fails her. She wonders where you are. It's time to open my first letter. She worries for a moment what I might have written about her. Maybe someone will fish it oily and dripping from the bay behind her. Maybe they'll take it seriously.

Your Loving Father,

THE EXCISE-MAN

"Freedom and Whisky gang thegither."

—ROBERT BURNS

There was Bill's still and store sacked and burned and salt sown there under the scabs those gouger bastards had left in the earth—just to make their point the clearer. It takes us a minute and then we figure the excise-man caught him at it, that Bill's in the dock by now, combing the lice out of the bailiff's hay, so we go down to the lockup in a lynching mood, but as yet undecided who it'd do best to string up: our Billie for being careless, the bumbailiff for being a friend to the King, or the excise-man himself, for whom no man would mourn.

So we march in and there's the bailiff taking his coffee with a spoon of the aqua vitae—pleased to see us, he says. And did you pay duty on that dram? I ask him. He makes like he's hard of hearing. I say, I said, did you pay your tax to His Royal So-forth when you bought your collaborator's dram?

I render unto Caesar, he answers back, and you'd do best to render too.

I'd flog my kiddies for so much as thinking of giving the throne its pound of flesh, I say, and there come hurrahs from some quarters, followed by calls for the stringing up of the bailiff there and then. It's in this edifying atmosphere that I then ask after Bill.

There's no Bill here, says the bailiff.

Bill, old Bill, Billie-boy, I say. The bailiff does a psalter's worth of swearing that there's no one by that name on the premises.

We'll be having a look around back, then, I say, and the bailiff says welcome to it. So around back we go, and there are the cells, and the same fat gouger bastard playing patience with the one arm on that same old wooden table, and minding his key-ring with the other; and there's the same Davey in the dock, who's been there thirty years, sitting on his bunk and opening the day's post from a thick spread of envelopes on the floor, the cream paper sooty with his footprints.

A lot of mail you've received, I say to Davey, to be friendly, but I suppose you've got the time now for correspondence. Tell me, if you've that many friends on the outside, why not get them together to go your bail?

Why not, indeed, some of my rowdier constituents inquire, ask your friends to storm the dock and bust you out?

I have no friends on the outside, gentlemen, says Davey. These letters come from the families of those who've suffered at my hand, and form the basis of my rehabilitation. I've been ordered by the court to make inquiries into my victims' ancestry, which naturally I must do through the post, not being allowed to leave the premises. The cost of my stamps is covered by a special charitable fund, and the bailiff says I'll get my parole when I find my way back to Eve and Adam.

That's a hell of a task, I say. Herculean.

You don't know the half of it, says Davey. These parish records are a disgrace.

What was it you did, again, to get sent up? I ask him. You've been in here long as I can remember.

Damned if I didn't kill twenty peddlers for their clothes and money. Not all at once, mind you, but over two years' time, sir, as they passed my house at the five-mile post.

Twenty peddlers! I cry. A prodigious feat for so young a boy.

It came to me so naturally, he says, I don't feel as I deserve your admiration.

And how go your inquiries? I ask. That is, how many of those peddlers' progenitors have you traced back to the Garden?

Just the one, says Davey.

And have you seen old Bill today? I ask.

He was in this morning, Davey says, but that devil of an excise-man came to take him out. He put Billie's neck in an iron brace and led him off like a dog, and Bill in nothing but what God gave him, screaming hello blue Jesus like he was bound for the bottom of the world.

I ask, Which way?

I'd advise against it, he says, but if you're bound and determined to follow, you might look by Roman Tom's house. It's as far as I saw them go from out my tiny window, and though he's a fucking Catholic, Tom would be no friend to the excise-man.

I give Davey our thanks and ask if he'd be interested in our stringing up the bailiff for him, but he says no, he'd like to get back to his work, even though all the ink in the jailhouse turned clear as water since the excise-man passed through. We leave the dock in peace and head up the hill to Roman Tom's, which is as uncongenial a place as you can imagine, with all his roof thatching and turf likewise white with bird droppings brittle as chalk, and shrill slaughtering-day sounds coming from inside his greasy walls. I knock on his door and out wafts the shriveled fellow in a white frock to ask my business. There are calls for the stringing up of Roman Tom there and then, but I ask, What goes on in there, Tom? Tell us, what's the awful din?

I'm plying my trade, he says, skittish. I make musical instruments, you know.

Music nothing, says I. Sounds like a flock of geese having their heads twisted off.

You're not far wrong, he says.

I'm not sure I follow you, is my reply.

It's simple, he says, and I can see that he's proud of his work. My commission is with the Holy Church. You can't use just any instrument in the Lord's house. A goose might do nicely, for starters. First you starve the bird till it's nearly hollow. If it's a bass voice you're wanting, the syrinx is treated with tar and copper. Two brass bowls of like proportion and density are stitched into the creature's trunk. The neck is telescoped to prevent rising tones, the wings and legs amputated to prevent atrophy and gangrene. Thereafter, water and fruit juice may be provided to sustain the creature, which ought to recuperate from the operation in about month's time. Result: a deep, resonant tone. So deep and resonant, in fact, that it's best to gag the beast when not in use, as the notes it produces have been known to cause toothache when sounded in too small a room. We have a whole flock of these set in vases lining the nave on Good Friday, and in that acoustical environment, the sounds are not only harmless but positively inspiring.

And if I'm in the market for a countertenor? I ask, joshing the man.

Neck and beak are lined in and out with gently curved iron fillings, he says. The neck is elongated to provide sustainable modulation. Three copper bells are strung across the interior of the chest-cavity, with wood and silk dampers strapped to the ribcage for arpeggio. Result: a bold, spirit-lifting clarity. As in the previous example, wings and legs are amputated to prevent atrophy and gangrene, and the animal should be gagged right away, once recovered, to prevent the perforation of eardrums and the loss of precious crystal if it should squawk in close quarters. These are for royal weddings, christenings, triumphal marches, and Easter Sunday.

You're a craftsman's craftsman and no mistake, says I, though I don't pretend to understand this fucking popery. But is it true that old Bill might've come by your land this morning?

Roman Tom nods, and I see that his head's as wan as a winter leaf: You'll call me a liar, he says, but not two hours ago, I swear I heard a voice very much like old Bill's, howling away like his ten toes were being served up for a Hottentot's tea. Yet when I looked out my window, all I saw was a man in a three-cornered hat and traveling cloak, carrying a kit bag and whistling "My Bonnie."

Devil of an excise-man, I say. He must've plunked Billie-boy in his rucksack.

I couldn't advise you to do so, Tom says, but if you're looking to catch up with the villain, I saw him heading up by Cooper's public house, with the grass going brown and dead beneath his feet—but as my two eyes are ruined from close work with the scalpel, that's all I can tell you with assurance.

So I thank the ignorant old cuss and tell him he isn't as rank a fucker as I'd heard, for which kindness he's suitably grateful, and we get a move on before he can start into preaching. Past the five-mile post we come to Cooper's pub and settle in to rest our feet. Cooper himself comes up, a man with a store of his own good whisky, a fine row of round brown spinsters up in his attic waiting to be courted. I see no one's watching and tap my nose, asking for a smuggler's dram and not the rinse on his shelf for show.

By no means, says Cooper, I've smashed all my barrels and pitched my bowthy into the swamp.

You what? is my cry, and there come calls for the stringing up of Cooper there and then. I ask what possessed him to do such a thing. Come up to the attic, he says, so it's up we go along stairs that whinge like horses giving birth to mules.

The attic is just as I remember it, with a good view of the good old town a good few miles back, and a sweet prickly mustiness like a lady's linen closet from the stuff heaped along the walls, once belonging to Cooper's packrat wife, dead now these six years of the dropsy. I say to Cooper I'm ready to hear his confession but he puts a finger over his womanish lips, goes to the corner, and damned if he doesn't pull down a ladder from the ceiling and climb on up and through.

This is the upper-attic, he tells me when I've gone after him, and I see there's a contraption the size of a cart and horse up there: an abacus crossed with an astrolabe crossed with teakettle, all whirling rings and bars and beads and hissing spouts. What in God's hell is it? I ask Cooper, and he pulls up a stool and sits and mops his brow with his apron, pulling it up to cover his hairless face.

It's my cross to bear, he says. It was my bounden duty to tend it and instead I turned my back. With my poor father dead in prison, I thought I had a right to marry and live a life like other men, you see, but I know now that this was vanity, only selfishness and vanity.

What is it, Cooper? I ask him again. This gadget, what's it for?

I can tell you that it controls the speed and rotation and position of the planet Mars, he says, just as surely as a hand crank on a well will bring up your bucket.

I tell Cooper that's a hard one to swallow, and he gets so huffy and cherry-faced I have to take a step back, though this means moving closer to the huge doohickey, which smells of grease and lye. A hard one to swallow! he cries. I'll tell you, this isn't the only public house in the low country with a planet-contraption, either. If Currie down the lane weren't cross-eyed with drink all seven days of the week, we'd have ourselves a full moon to see by every night, all year round, like a second sun! And don't you say to me you've never noticed the conduct of the girlies down at Knox's house, which I know to have power over lustful Venus . . .

I did notice it, at that, I say back, and now that you're mentioning it, I've always been curious why it was that so many brawls do occur here under your own fine roof, Mister Cooper. Could it be the influence of warlike Mars?

That it is, says Cooper, and it was the devil's own luck brought my family into the employment of that vindictive, bloodshot eyeball in the sky.

Could you not give it up? I ask him, Sell the house, if you find the burden too great?

Give it up? he asks, and looks like he might smash me one. The maintenance of such a fine piece of machinery—and to strangers? I myself was born to tend this contraption. I inherited it from my poor dad, and look what a mess I've made of it! I abandoned my post for near twenty years to raise a family and make my own whisky. Mars went roaming around the firmament looking for trouble, bringing wars all over the world and no end to the fuss. I have to make up for my sins and keep her well oiled and running smooth from here on in.

My question then, I say to Cooper, is which public house has a planet-contraption for this, our very own star? Who is it keeps us a good distance from Mars or Venus—or from our sun himself, for that matter?

That I do not know, says Cooper, looking thoughtful. But don't think I haven't pondered it. My theory is that the machines operate upon a principle of reciprocity, that all the lights in the sky are counterbalanced like weights on a scale: that much as the Martians and Venusians are our responsibility, and the Lunatics and Saturnians as well, we poor human men are in the care of some publican located on one of those planets, or one farther still from our home, member of a nation as yet unknown to us. We can only pray that the party in question is less willful than myself, or blind Currie, or even poor slobbering Knox, and keeps ourselves in mind as he goes about his business, and takes care we don't go careening through hell and creation like I've let old Mars do in my years of decadence.

Tell me then, Cooper, if Venus makes us venereal, and Saturn saturnine, what power does our own earth exert upon the peoples of those other stars?

Cooper was pale as he replied, I can only speculate. But it is undoubtedly a most dreadful condition.

Then God bless you and your endeavors, I say. And best of luck to you and your brother contraptioners. Before

I leave you to your vocation, however, is it possible you've seen our Bill today?

With all the sweat and blood I pour into my machine, it's a wonder I have time to pour the drinks downstairs, says poor Cooper, who squints at his apparatus like a young wife at her old knock-kneed husband. But now that you've mentioned it, I can tell you that there was queer business afoot here this morning. I came into the common room at supper and saw a man dressed in black silk and a tricorne, like a rich country cleric, with a leather handle-bag full of such strange equipage as even a celestial mechanic like myself's never seen—which he says is all for weighing and measuring, but looked to me like what you'd find in a pasha's torture chamber. He's sipping at the King's whisky, and I ask him if he'll want some vittles along with his drink, and he says, all polite, "No and thank you, sir, for I've just eaten well and full, and could not touch me another bite." "And where did you get your breakfast, sir?" I ask the gentleman, thinking maybe there's some competition brewing in the neighborhood, and he tells me straight out that he's just supped on the skin of a sinner named Bill.

He ate up our Bill? I shout.

The very devil of an excise-man, says Cooper. He lit out then for Sherrie's cathouse, which sits outside the township entire, and all my milk soured as soon as he'd gone.

I know my way to Sherrie's cathouse, I say, and thank Cooper again for his time. Down I climb back to the attic-proper and then the pub-proper and rally my mob back to the hunt. The cathouse had been a manor once, which sat on a whole estate like a hen in her brood, but is weather-wracked and tilted now, and as crooked, they say, as Dame Sherrie herself. Up we go and ring for someone, but the sounds in the house are of lamentation and misery rather than merrymaking. Sherrie herself comes down, all made up like a dolly, though no tart herself, and wide as a hayrick.

We're closed for business, boys, she says to us.

Could it be there's something the matter, Sherrie? I ask her.

We've got ourselves some trouble, she says.

Is one of your girls with child? I ask her.

If only it were just the one, she says. So I ask is it two or three, and she laughs without cheer, like a farmer who's seen his crop black with locusts. Not two and not three, but *all*, my fine mister, and our livelihood wrecked into the bargain.

How is it possible? I ask. Not *all*, surely?

All, Sherrie tells me, every last fine girl in my house with child, and but one man come by since Sunday.

Only one? I ask. Tell us who, Dame Sherrie. It might make you feel better if we were to string him up without delay.

It was the excise-man, says Sherrie, none other, and him not gone an hour's time.

The excise-man! I hiss more than say. You took the excise-man's money? You let him lie with every last one of your girls?

Sherrie quakes and bids me to bite my tongue. I wouldn't let an excise-man in my house, as you shouldn't need telling. I told him to keep walking. And he said good day to me, all polite, but no sooner did he head into the wood than my girls all swelled like sheep in the sun.

Devil of an excise-man, I say. And you tell me he's gone into the wood?

Right on in, Sherrie says, and a great wailing fills our ears. She peeks her head inside the door and comes back shooing us away. Good God, she tells us, they've all come to term and given birth! There'll be an army of gougers coming down those steps in an instant—each full-grown, with pike and musket, and a match for your mob if I'm any judge.

So we take Sherrie's good advice and head out without delay to the other end of the wood, savage and thirsty for the blood of the excise-man. There's an old soldier-man there polishing his buttons and he tips his hat and says how do.

Davey! I cry. It's old Davey, isn't it? Give us a kiss—you're a free man! And not a day gone by since I left you in the lock-up, back in the good old town!

It's a peculiar thing, says Davey. David is my name, all right, but you have the advantage of me. I can't say I've ever made your acquaintance, sir, nor your friends here who gnash their teeth and look as like to string a gent up as pass the time of day.

Davey! I cry. Old Davey! Did you finish your inquiries and get rehabilitated, then?

I did at that, says Davey, though it took me forty years,

and I lost two fingers on my right hand from writing those letters all day and all night. Then the bailiff went and collected my correspondence into ten volumes of history and theology and published them in London under his own name.

And the town, old Davey, you prodigy, I say. Tell us about the good old town.

There's nothing good about it, he says. Fifty gouger bastards with pike and spear came swarming down the hill some dark morning and slew every man, woman, and child for whisky-distillers and smugglers. The English themselves came next, swarming over every stone and shrub, numbering each in black and red ink. They dug up the churchyard and pulled out the trees and put their spoils on carts, wood and bone and rock. There's no town left, and all because our bailiff confided to the mayor that a gang was out trying to lynch the crown's own excise-man.

So my mob and I put out a great lamentation of our own, and there come calls for the stringing up of ourselves there and then. In a flash my mob is hanging from two-dozen trees, leaving no one but Davey and myself on terra firma.

And the excise-man? I ask him, eager. What of the excise-man himself?

Transferred to another township, says Davey. Through the valley and out the other end. I saw him pass, all in sackcloth, and with him were ten wild hounds that looked at me sadly from blue eyes like men's. The excise-man tipped his hat to me, and damned if he didn't look for the world like our own Billie-boy, who left the good old town when I was still at His Majesty's service, stuck in the dock for my many crimes.

So what could I do but thank old Davey, leaving him at his buttons, and go on into the valley, gnashing my teeth, nothing on my mind but the stringing up of that old devil of an excise-man.

KURT VONNEGUT AND THE GREAT BORDELLOS OF THE DANUBE DELTA

How tedious it is to dream of the same person every night! It's exhausting: there's that face again, the two eyes (or that's how I remember her), the one mouth (I think I have that right?), the cheeks and pointy chin. Wanting to treat myself, to have a little vacation, I decided to stay awake through Thursday morning. When I opened my door and stepped out into the light of the smoldering trees, I knew I would see something different than would greet me having slept.

Who they are I couldn't tell you, but they're out there in the day, getting places, going places, moving their feet one after the other, moving forward without plans. To get anywhere I need a scheme, I need to see the reasons for lifting my feet; I need to see the route I'll take, the lines there and the different though likely parallel lines back. Still, and sparing myself nothing, I thought that today at last might be the moment to revive my abandoned project of preserving for my children the particulars of the great bordellos of the Danube Delta.

I've had the above sentences written for several months, and haven't been able to make up my mind quite what to do with them. Do they belong in a piece of fiction? I'd like it if they did. What a waste, if not. Did I sit and type those one hundred and eighty-six words for my health? How is it I can be no more certain than you of what my intentions were?

The sentences do carry the marks of fictiveness: there is an "I," but a certain sort of "I," the sort that refers—I think—to a different fellow than the unitalicized I beginning the paragraph preceding this. And yet, the Italic I above says many things the I who now addresses you might well say under some peculiar duress. There isn't a single sentence—save the last, and perhaps the bit about the trees—that I can really disavow: Here am I, and thus am I disposed. The last sentence reads as having been conceived in desperation, I think. The author is hoping to launch himself into fiction from a less than ideal altitude. Where does this conceit come from? Have the creeks risen?

But what is fiction, if not this peculiar duress? (If I am to write fiction, shouldn't I be able to identify some of its attributes?)

An anecdote: I remember lying beneath a gummy pool table in my youth, under the influence of certain substances it would I think be too vulgar to name, expositing at length from this position on the likely fate of the character of Ringo from the Lorne Green song of the same name ("A dozen guns spit fire and lead / A moment later, he lay dead")—hypothesizing that, having faked his death, the demonic gunfighter had wandered the earth until, at last, he found redemption in Jimmy Dean's "Big John" ("a crashing blow from a huge right hand / sent a Louisiana fella to the promised land"), having adopted, of course, an alias. Now, I am not given to spontaneity or improvisation. I wish I could remember how I came to my asinine conclusions. It must have been that the peculiar duress of whatever substances I'd ingested forced together the words of other men already extant in my memory, resulting in what I can only call a work of fiction, however derivative. Today, however, there is only the quotidian pressure exerted on my vocabulary—to the extent that it is mine—by the necessities of living among and communicating with the men and women in my proximity; and then the new trivia I take in, willingly or unwillingly, from books, movies, songs, eavesdropping. To write, then, and to write fiction, we must adopt a means (stolen) to deform our casual vocabularies (inherited) in order to include or exclude those words we hope will, by their presence or absence, achieve one or another effect (imitated). Does that sound workable, to you? Is that a productive place to begin?

I have around one hundred and eighty words, a couple of paragraphs that I'd like to "flesh out," to rescue. I'd like to make something out of this stew that will be—what?—satisfying, that will affect a reader as the writing I admire has affected me. I do not even, at this stage, want to make something pretty; I do not even, at this stage, want to add something of value to the world. Really, what hope is there of that? The world is everything that is in no need of me. But writers write, whether or not they are constructing anything worth the species' while. (This is what they call a tautology.) No point trying to stop them, goodness knows.

I am a trusting sort, and so am likely to turn to my betters for help. And though it's been a few years now since I was officially enrolled in an academic program meant in some undefined way to address my aspiration to write fiction, it is easy enough to ask around for a refresher, since it seems—or haven't you noticed?—that, given the now-invisible demarcation between writer and teacher of writing, virtually every author of note, be they professional or professor, has issued a choice few squibs as to the rudiments of their productivity. Indeed, the number of "rules for writing" on record continue to proliferate. Given that these deca-, hepta-, pentalogs, craft essays, and meditations are written exclusively by writers—QED—they must have a legitimate claim to being a literary form in themselves. A form, I'll say, of fiction—what's a polemic but a work of fiction? what's a fiction but a form of rhetoric?—to which we may respond, of which we may produce analyses. Let me pick one more or less at random. They tend to have elements in common, these fictions. They tend to have assumptions in common. I will assume you have seen one or two in your time.

Why not pick on poor Kurt Vonnegut. Do you remember Kurt Vonnegut? Mr. Vonnegut has left us eight rules for writing, in the introduction to his short-story collection *Bagombo Snuff Box*. Why shouldn't I rely on Mr. Vonnegut to help me find my way back to the Danube Delta, since I seem to have gotten myself lost? (Am I being unreasonable?)

1. Use the time of a total stranger in such a way that he or she will not feel the time was wasted.

But: Is the above statement about fiction? How can I *use* anyone's time, let alone a total stranger's? Am I using my own? Right now? Am I *wasting* it? And how can I gauge what will or will not seem like a waste of said time to someone so very, so totally strange? Do they enjoy reading? Would they perhaps prefer a game of cards? Should I ask them if they would like to play a game of cards with me rather than read some abstruse piece of fiction that, for whatever reason, probably neurotic, I have been pleased to *use* my own time writing? I am no closer to adding any words to my little stockpile. Please advise.

2. Give the reader at least one character he or she can root for.

The verbs here are mystifying, but the nouns, too, no walk in the park. (Parks are where you walk, *n'est-ce pas*?) First I was using what did not belong to me, the time of my totally strange reader; now I am expected to *give* them something—something, I suppose, in exchange for that time. Well, that seems fair, inasmuch as I understand commerce. But what character am I supposed to give them? Whose character? *I* have no character to speak of. Of course, I'm familiar with the notion that readers are often fondest of books in which the proper nouns are described in such a way that they can, perhaps accidentally—against their will?—mistake these nouns for absent human beings . . . but not a word from Mr. Vonnegut as to how one manages this trick. And note the assumption that playing this trick is inherently desirable . . . and all this before we reach that troublesome verb "root." Is it not enough that we so mystify our readers that they mistake nouns for living men and women? Now, too, our readers must "root" for these phantoms? We must *sympathize* with our nouns? I could hardly deny that they're important—our kissing cousins—but what, then, of the other parts of speech? Are they to remain unloved? Prepositions are far more piquant and individual than nouns, since they point to no practical definitions. Might we not have a preposition as a hero? I would root for a preposition.

But the answer must be: We give readers a character to root for so that we are not *using* their time irresponsibly. There is something unsavory about the transaction Mr. Vonnegut is recommending.

3. Every character should want something, even if it is only a glass of water.

We are up to number three, and nothing at all has been said about writing. But here, at least, I feel I can make sense of the "rule." If we are to *root* for a given character, then that character, like we ourselves, must on occasion want a glass of water—or, to be precise, must be described as wanting the words denoting a glass of water, and be described either enjoying or being denied said description of said glass. *My* character, my Italic I, does seem to want something, though what this something might be is unclear. Perhaps what he wants is to want something clear (clear, you see, like a glass of water, unless you're reading this on Staten Island). Perhaps if I had written my sentences entirely about this desire for clarity—with which we can all, as mammals, I believe, identify—then I would not be in this predicament. I would know how to finish my fiction. If it is a fiction.

Anecdote II: I was friendly once (well, more than once) with a person who was teaching a writing workshop. A student of hers, who was going blind, degeneratively, genetically, permanently, submitted a short story to the class that was, as I recall, a list of instructions as to how the reader could, similarly, achieve a state of blindness, written as though this was inherently desirable: Here, ladies and gentleman, are some inside tips on blindness from Someone Who Knows. My teacher-friend complained that this was not a good story because not believable: Who would *want* to go blind?

I do not want to go blind, friend. It seems I don't much want to go anywhere anymore. And I don't see *how* words want, or *what* words want. I know, however, that I *do* want to read a story that wants me to want to go blind. I want to root for a story that wants me to want something I could not possibly want.

Do you believe that I want this? Are you rooting for me?

4. Every sentence must do one of two things—reveal character or advance the action.

At last there is mention of a basic unit of prose: the sentence. I may not know how to make characters who want things, but I am confident that I know how to make sentences. A sentence, perhaps, like "Jeremy thought, shivering at his desk, with a space heater lamenting over his toes, how much he would like to write a story about a character wanting a glass of water." This sentence reveals something about the character of Jeremy. This sentence advances the action of my story. My story will be about a character named Jeremy, who wants to write a story about a character wanting a glass of water. Perhaps this unnamed character teaches a writing workshop. Thirsty work, unquestionably. This unnamed character's students all want to write stories about characters who want, badly, to go blind. They do not want glasses of water, but never to see. Blindness trumps thirst. We are cooking now, Mr. Vonnegut. I will call this story, "The Great Bordellos of the Danube Delta," for reasons that are wholly mysterious to me.

5. Start as close to the end as possible.

Here I begin to wonder whether this is all a prank. Shall we argue about how close to the end of a piece of fiction we may begin before it must end? Wouldn't the end itself be the closest point to the end? Might the ending not then take ten pages, or twenty, or seven hundred to end? Could it be that Mr. Vonnegut would rather we not write fiction at all? He is trying to rescue us from something nasty, I suspect. He has our best interests at heart. Should we not listen? He always seemed like a nice guy.

6. Be a sadist. No matter how sweet and innocent your leading characters, make awful things happen to them—in order that the reader may see what they are made of.

So much for niceness. But what *are* these leading characters made of? And where have they come from, these singularly helpless homunculi? And note the assumption that they must begin sweet and innocent. All the better to root for. "When you bake your cake, make sure the pickles are turquoise." This is probably excellent advice. For something.

7. Write to please just one person.

The second reference to the activity of writing. But how to please our one person? What does she want? Does she want a glass of water, or does she want a novel? It would be easier to give her a glass of water. But perhaps she can get it herself.

8. Give your readers as much information as possible as soon as possible. . . . Readers should have such complete understanding of what is going on, where and why, that they could finish the story themselves.

I only know as much as one hundred and eighty or so words of italicized text can tell me about my story. That is every bit of information available. Wait, I will try to give you more. I will even try to follow the rules.

It was almost over, I was nearly beaten . . . but not quite! Still I wanted, needed, to persevere, to the very end, which was close—I could feel it. I ignored the notes and calls and flares and codes from the people who used to care about me. They can't help me now, and I can't help them: Look what I've turned into. They don't see my walking, which is self-conscious and lopsided, or else they'd have given me up. God but I'm thirsty.

Who would think a man like me had once waded through mud and wire, searching in vain for your mother in one after another of the great bordellos of the Danube Delta?

Finish up for me? I would be grateful. Play your cards right and you'll get a byline.

It would seem natural, even inevitable, to assume that writers asked to make recommendations about writing will recommend that one produce writing similar to their own. Or, anyway, this would seem a natural conclusion were we discussing a fictional character. Fictional characters have motives, as we all know, and these motives can be pithily summarized, and tend to be consistent. (Alternatively, they have motives that are inscrutable, in which case they will generally have an author to whom we can attribute such a motive, much as we would with a fictional character: the writer has decided, you see, to author a piece of fiction demonstrating that all character is unknowable, and is doing her best to be consistent.) And yet, taking Mr. Vonnegut's rules (unfairly, and out of context, I grant you) as emblematic of the "friendly advice" often disseminated to writers in the guise (likewise unfair) of pedagogy, it is hard to see what lessons, save brevity, could be learned here. I could not even, following these rules, approximate Mr. Vonnegut's style.

If I were to speculate as to Mr. Vonnegut's "real" motives in writing his list—if I were to psychoanalyze him; that is, if I were to treat him as *my* fictional character—I would assume that his eight dictums referred to particular prescriptions employed in Mr. Vonnegut's own fiction that he either

- felt likely to abandon at any moment: the temptation to begin nearer the middle or to write about a character with no identifiable motives being so terrible that he was obliged to warn others away; or else
- admired to the exclusion of that which we might call *writing*, and which he believed were near enough the secret of his success that he could offer no aid so effective to amateurs enamored of his work than a summary thereof.

It is interesting to note that, taken as an independent work of fiction, Mr. Vonnegut's rules obey their own precepts, more or less, while many if not all of his novels do not. What are his characters made of? Look and see. Not even air.

If we take Mr. Vonnegut's list of rules as a work of fiction, does it "contain" characters? I believe so: there is Mr. Vonnegut himself, or the narrator impersonating him, and then too his addressee, for whom these recommendations are intended: an imaginary writer-in-training forearmed with all the proper points of reference for decoding Mr. Vonnegut's modest proposals. Likewise, our cast contains the unborn sentences to be written by our fictional writer, following Mr. Vonnegut's advice, and then this fictional writer's prospective fictional characters, who will "inhabit" these fictional, as-yet-unwritten sentences—and of course the much-desired glass of water, which might even be our protagonist; and then, how could we forget the mysterious and rather sexy "total stranger"? These characters' attributes are implied by our (unreliable?) narrator's assumptions: they are not depicted. And why should they be? The players are familiar. They caper so pleasantly it's easy to forget they are stock characters. "Character" instead of Pierrot, "Reader" instead of Harlequin. It takes such a little dose of naïveté, or perhaps of suspicion, to show how little we—or I?—actually know about these old friends; how little use they are, save for the fictional writer to whom these rules were addressed, and for whom I suspect we are meant to root.

But I don't mean to sound censorious. It isn't (entirely) my intention to make Mr. Vonnegut into a fictional character upon whom I may practice my own authorial sadism. He himself says, after all, that "great" writers break his rules all the time. (Which statement raises more questions than it answers, in terms of his motives in writing those rules to begin with—but never mind.) There are other such lists and other successful writers I could have chosen. It is interesting to note that Elmore Leonard, a writer understood (no, I can't substantiate this claim) to be less "literary" than Vonnegut, has written rules that are far more practical, far more likely to be of use to a beginning fiction writer; he tells us, for instance, to avoid exclamation points, adverbs, and ostentatious dialogue tags. Mr. Leonard is not practicing some sort of divination, but instructing us to write economical prose economically. This is refreshing. Still, you'll find that Mr. Leonard sums up his rules with the statement: **IF IT SOUNDS LIKE WRITING, I REWRITE IT.** This is meant to be provocative and sensible both, and yet the cognitive—and logical—dissonance here is such that one might as well be riddling with the Mad Hatter. Is this, I've always wondered, a joke? But no, I am being asked to write the unwritten, to unwrite my writing, and this is intended as sensible advice. Yet one presumes Mr. Leonard does does not mean to encourage his disciples to follow in the footsteps of, for example, Maurice Blanchot.

Is all instruction on the subject of writing simply the composition of short[1] fictions on the subject of writing—consistent or contradictory, plainspoken or theoretical, "realistic" or autocritical? The sentences that writers in and out of the mainstream use to approach their—what?—craft,

1. Or long? Let us never forget Ms. Stein's more than admirable, even prophetic, contribution to the genre, perhaps its apotheosis: *How to Write*.

and to transmit ideas about fiction, to teach and even to grapple with the problems their own fictions are presenting them at a given moment, seem to amount, in the main, to platitudes, allegories, fairy tales about writing . . . and, Mr. Leonard aside, the closer one hews to what we like to call realism in one's work—or one's rhetoric about one's work—the more likely one is to speak in florid alchemical metaphor when attempting to give another writer the benefit of your wisdom. ("You have to love before you can be relentless."[2] But Stendhal, as ever, had the right idea: first teach us how to love, Mr. Author, if you're such a smarty-pants; then, if there's time, maybe we'll talk about books.) Unbelievable that fiction, still, to teachers of fiction, is a dollhouse in which to stage-manage suffering effigies.

Then again, perhaps I do wrong to dismiss this notion out of hand. If we pretend for a moment that fictional characters are indeed independent entities—as it seems so many writers must do in order to speak coherently—might it be that the motive shared by each of them, the desire that is common to every such "individual," is the desire *not* to be a part of a work of fiction? To escape our scrutiny, our language? To reach "the end"? This—at least in the fiction about fiction you are reading now—strikes me as the only plausible possibility. "The split between sensation and thinking is not a 'frame of reference.' . . . It is actually quite

2. Jonathan Franzen, in the *Guardian*. http://www.guardian.co.uk/books/2010/feb/20/ten-rules-for-writing-fiction-part-one

painful,"[3] as someone once said. When we imagine the men and women described by the words in a piece of fiction, we are imagining subjects perched precisely on this unbearable fault line. No wonder that otherwise intelligent people tend to stumble into nonsense when trying to define them. I take back what I said about words wanting: the only joy of any proper noun, surely, is to be predicated and full-stopped. Part of our pleasure in reading is the joy of the suspension and then execution of our nouns' last wishes. Words do not die intestate. We *know* what they want. They want to be done.

Why not venture, humbly, a few rules for the writer of rules of writing, if you're such a smarty-pants, Mr. Writer? Or, better still, questions. Questions will better define the skeptical character of the imaginary man or woman serving here as my narrator:

1. **Is it an aid to the writing of fiction to be told to think or not think a certain way about the writing of fiction?**
2. **Is it an aid to the writing of fiction to be told in what way to live your life or organize your habits while writing or contemplating the writing of a work of fiction?**

3. Charles Newman. *The Post-Modern Aura* (Evanston, IL: Northwestern Univ. Press, 1985) 83.

3. **Is it an aid to the writing of fiction to be told to read everything, or to read certain things, or to avoid reading certain things, or to avoid reading at all?**
4. **Is it an aid to the writing of fiction to be told how other writers of fiction write their fiction?**
5. **Is it an aid to the writing of fiction to have the desired results of a prospective work of fiction described as one would an object or effect in a work of fiction?**
6. **A poet has written,** "A poem written in pen could never have been written in pencil."[4] **Do you agree that this also applies to the writing of prose?**

And I suspect that asking questions is the best, probably the only means of addressing our need to write fictions. Fiction can be many things, and no one mode is inappropriate for it—no one genre, no one method, no one orthodoxy, no one heresy, no matter my own prejudices—but it may be accurate to describe it, as many have done, as essentially a form of attention, attention specifically to language, attention even to the "absent friends" we can make believe that this language describes: which is why the novel form recedes as far back into history as we are likely to go looking for it. Fiction is a mode of thought; it is inherent to our thinking. I have a mind, I think, when I write fiction; the rest of the time, I'm not so sure. The rest of the time, I have *behavior.*

4. Ron Silliman. *The Chinese Notebook.* Collected in *The Age of Huts (Compleat).* (Berkley: Univ. of California Press, 2007) 171.

I am balanced between my own unconsidered uses of language and those of my society.

How bloodless. How parsimonious. How neurotic. But I believe all good fiction—and I mean *all*; regardless of trope or era or school, realist or non, mainstream or underground—has this in common: a skepticism as to the possibility of writing fiction. I do not ask myself, "What is fiction?" though I do on occasion wonder *if* there is fiction, and this skepticism is absent from Mr. Vonnegut's rules. I can't say I've ever found it in this strange literary form that we have been discussing. Which may be, in part, why it is so unsatisfying to the skeptical.

If we mean to teach ourselves how to write, to teach others how to write, we must make clear what it is we mean to learn, and in our (I think) inevitable failure to do this, perhaps undermine the notion that fiction is a certain, indispensible, enlightened practice. If there is an enemy, in the land of fiction, it is not any of our -isms, parts of speech, or narratorial strategies, but habit and presumption. Rules of fiction writing build upon an axiom that we must never take as read[5]: that fiction may be written.

To believe overmuch in Literature is to invest our sympathies in a character no more tangible than Billy Pilgrim, Enkidu, or Richard Nixon.

(And to believe in it too little is to court the "minor.")

5. Joke.

Here is one account of the process in which I can find no fault:

"I write sentences. I write first one sentence, then another sentence. I write sentence after sentence. . . . I write a hundred or more sentences each week and a few thousand sentences a year. . . . After I've written each sentence I read it aloud. I listen to the sound of the sentence, and I don't begin to write the next sentence unless I'm absolutely satisfied with the sound of the sentences I'm listening to. . . . When I've written a paragraph I read it aloud to learn whether all the sentences that sounded well on their own still sound well together."[6]

Which is to say that there's no help to be had. Not for me, not for any aspirant. We will have to crawl our way out of this sludge sentence by sentence. We'll have to graze our knuckles on every inch of bitter punctuation. And to what end, we will wonder, and go on wondering, as our shoes fill with water and mud, the world capsizes around us, and still we don't desist.

People move from point to point as though the world were nothing but places they could be. Me, I can walk up and down my street and wave to the firemen, but I know what I'm seeing is somewhere nothing could live.

6. Gerald Murnane. *Invisible Yet Enduring Lilacs* (Artamon, New South Wales: Giramondo Publishing, 2005) 25.

One street in particular attracts more than its share of rats. Walking there with someone is a gamble; some people shriek, and the noise is embarrassing before the rare unbroken window.

Were I to meet anyone now, though they wouldn't know me, I'd be unable to keep from telling them the story of my first days as a paying customer, wrapped tightly in reeds, my hair papered with leaves, clotted stiff and itching in the master bed of one of the many great bordellos of the Danube Delta.

THE SINCES

Since you went away, I have not been ill so much as a day.

Since you went away, I go to bed hungry and wake up nauseatingly full.

Since you went away, I've realized that one can never ask an intimate for the basic courtesy one would unthinkingly extend to a stranger.

Since you went away, I find myself wondering how much longer there will be a London, a New York, a hot shower for me in the morning.

Since you went away, I have less resistance to the temptation to write entirely in repetitive declarations, which in their lack of adornment give an illusion of economy and development.

Since you went away, I wonder whether it is a failure on my part or an essential feature of our relationship that any plain account of it I write tends unerringly toward the character of kitsch.

Since you went away, I have an increased interest in Marxism; by which I mean it has become all the more attractive to me to be the sort of person who would be able to apply themselves to the procedure of educating themselves about Marxism.

Since you went away, I've found myself thinking, for the

first time in years, of the flatulent dog belonging to the last woman who lived with me, and of whom I once said, in a spirit close to that of "automatic writing," that he had a handsome profile.

Since you went away, I notice that there's an exceptional amount of dust in my living space, under chairs and in corners and on dressers and between books and over countertops, and very likely in other places where it's still, mercifully, invisible to me; leading me to wonder whether it's possible that I'm now disintegrating at an accelerated rate.

Since you went away, it isn't so much you that I miss, though I'll admit that I missed you badly enough initially, as the *likelihood* of you, in the terms, for instance, of a system or engine or procedure that, because of the wear on some minute but necessary component—a bulb, a piece of string, an argument, washer, or gear—can no longer be made to function: it is not, therefore (strictly speaking) a *personal* loss.

Since you went away, I dream often of the end of the world; but by this I mean an end only to the comforts I still have in life, and the replacement of my familiar abstract distresses with the more acute ones represented by exposure to the elements, fighting for subsistence, resocialization into a community to which I can offer even less than I do the nominally civil, protective one I'm a member of now; that is, I often have nightmares.

Since you went away, my hands shake, or more precisely my fingers, or more precisely one of my three center fingers, most especially the pointer or ring—or else they vibrate, back and forth, or do I mean describe an ellipse, in a manner I find it impossible to duplicate intentionally; although, watching this as it occurs, without intention, and in spite of my alarm, in spite of my desire to stop, I find the performance impressive; that is, though it alarms me, I recognize that it's a neat trick.

Since you went away, and with our home nearly vacant of furniture, wall-hangings, animals, burglars, or other sonic buffers, and being as it is constructed of old, thin, cheap, brittle, and improperly insulated wood—which I tend to prefer, I admit, despite the disadvantages, but which, more to the point, had hoped you would approve of—the sounds of the upstairs neighbors' fucking is so audible as to be comic; or, rather, *would* be comic if it didn't evoke in me, mechanically, before I can think twice, the most basic, petrifying, juvenile reaction imaginable; namely, "He's hurting her!"

Since you went away, I find it difficult to remember the layout of the room we once shared: its slanted ceiling, the little chair seemingly foreshortened in a corner made inaccessible by said slant; no one could fit on it except the cat we didn't have; and my nightstand, on which I kept a copy of Stendhal's *On Love*, my place marked with an illegible unfinished handwritten note from another woman, to whom I had never been able to make love, written with a spilling steel nib on expensive paper purchased some years earlier on the Lower East Side from a store since forgotten though often searched for: the name escapes her.

Since you went away, I have—due in some measure I'm sure to my living in a new town, a new building, in a new atmosphere and environment—lost whatever measure of gracefulness had previously obtained in my dealings with the inanimate world, be it represented by doorknobs, counters, cabinets, shelves, spoons, bowls, teacups, or even level spans of floorboard; I am ungainly, I trip, I catch my clothes on the most innocuous, rounded, unthreatening bumps; I sigh too much, I seem unable to undertake the simplest perambulation without endless recursions to retrieve or mop or sweep up what I've dropped or spilled or broken in transit; and, tired, irritated with my clumsiness, I waddle, room to room, lifting my feet so little that I am bound, again, to stumble, and soon.

Since you went away, in fact, I find I am able to blame virtually all my longstanding personal problems on your absence—though in their respective advents they predate your departure, our affair, and perhaps even our first meeting by months or years—namely: I am lethargic; I find it impossible to accomplish even simple tasks that would appreciably improve the standard of my day-to-day life (going to the Laundromat, getting my car fixed, buying food, buying bug-spray); no one calls; I masturbate too often (if someone called, I suppose, it would at least provide an interruption), and joylessly at that; I eat out too much, and eat too much while out; I spend too much money on books and then have difficulty concentrating when I read . . . extend until desired length is achieved.

Since you went away, I have wondered whether I might be doing humanity a service, or simply reiterating the rudiments of a procedure already familiar to worldly adults but only belatedly discovered by myself, in making public my as-yet foolproof means of hiding the fact that you have invited another woman or man into the bed you habitually share with your cohabitant, on such occasions that it would seem suspicious and indeed out of character to launder the sheets and pillowcases and blankets the latter woman or man last saw on the bed before perhaps leaving town to spend the weekend with her or his family; namely, to prepare a weak solution of the latter man or woman's shampoo or conditioner and a brittle sliver of his or her deodorant in cold water and sprinkle said pillowcases and sheets and blankets with this reagent so as to give the ensemble a scent not unlike the usual nighttime miasma found thereupon during those weeks when you were still faithful.

Since you went away, I can't clean anything—which is not to say that I *do not* clean anything, though my indolence in this respect is becoming a religion to which I am tempted to devote the remainder of my faith; but only that what I *do* clean, when I clean it, what I focus myself on cleaning, be it a dish or a shelf or an area of floor, *resists* being cleaned: that however long I devote to the process of cleaning it or them, it or they remain dirty after I'm finished, after it or they and I endure what I would previously have considered a sufficient if not excessive span of cleaning time: that there is always a speck or spot or stain remaining; the question being, now, whether I have grown incapable of completing even this simple act to my own satisfaction, or whether my attention or critical faculty has finally and decisively outstripped my talent, leaving me with a genius for the *perception* of filth but only an average, mediocre talent for remedying it.

Since you went away, I find, when alone, that I am more and more unable to control my verbalizations at certain thankfully brief moments; and, further, that I can't even begin to essay a description of my state of mind at such moments, since despite their entirely verbal and thus textual effect on my physiology (in that the only definable result of this "attack" is speech), there seems—by contrast to virtually every other moment of my life, waking or sleeping—to be very little that is syntactical or paraphraseable in my thoughts when so affected, uttering a stream of (usually three, paramount) obscenities, "cunt" chief among them, before recovering my self-control and praying (praying is precisely the word) that no one nearby has heard me, and praying too (this is the crux of the matter) that my condition doesn't degenerate beyond this stage, envisioning myself (as is only natural) having such a "fit" in polite company: my anxiety here running down two channels, parallel and simultaneous, one of concern for my own well-being (am I losing my mind? is this a harbinger of other and worse pathologies?) and one, stronger—overwhelming, in fact—of terror at the prospect of my humiliation.

Since you went away, I've noticed an attraction on my part toward writing that purports to be honest, or purports to be an attempt at honesty, or in particular that is not constructed around the obligation toward situations, movements, activities within the liminal space of fiction ("Please imagine this place, and these people, who will do or say things to one another . . ."); despite a conviction (which seems only natural, indeed endemic) that all expression is counterfeit; therefore, I might characterize this "motion toward honesty" as the development of a peculiar taste—one in a long line of peculiar tastes, be they literary, musical, sensual, or culinary—for the *result* of writing that adopts, mendaciously, the *style* of honesty, and of a particularly *written* honesty, as opposed to writing that mimes (intentionally, thanks to technique, or unintentionally, thanks to incompetence) the character of inarticulate speech, the better to defuse a reader's assumption that what he or she is reading was composed in cold blood; in other words, in what I will call my decline, I have noticed a curious attraction on my part to writing that, in addition to working in defiance or ignorance of the nominal, ludic possibilities of fiction, is composed in ignorance or defiance of the to me transparent impossibility of writing a *direct chronicle*, if not *memoir*—an admission I am somewhat embarrassed to make.

That is, since you went away, I'm aging.

III.

ON THE FURTIVENESS OF KURTZ

1.

It has been much remarked upon. By those who have observed him. He's sitting. He's crouching. Crouching as though expecting a blow. Or else: As though recovering from a blow. Yes, so bent in his sitting that one could believe the blow's already fallen. I think: Characteristic of him to look as though expecting or else recovering from an attack. I think: Characteristic of him to sit in such a way as to invite an attack. I think: How best attack this Kurtz?

He is sitting with a woman, or not with a woman, isn't that a reasonable observation? And just where he's sitting is where he usually sits, crouched or near enough to crouching over his mug or cup or glass (this is dependent, the vessel, on season and time of day). He comes here often, and often sits where he now sits, as I am often sitting where I'm now sitting, indulging in a little anacoluthon (my doctor tells me no, but what's life, I ask, without these little pleasures?) when he comes in. When he comes in, he's often accompanied by a woman, who perhaps struck up a conversation with him on their first meeting by asking, "Do you come here often?"

He doesn't walk so much as he scuttles—is that fair of me to say? Kurtz prizes fairness, I imagine, because he perceives that he is not often treated fairly.

Where did you learn to say of men that they scuttle? he would ask.

I'd confess: The verb certainly comes from a book I once read about a man or woman who was meant by the author to seem distasteful.

But didn't it occur to you, reading this book, Kurtz would ask, that such a verb is hardly in the spirit of plain-dealing? Didn't it occur to you that to say of a man that he scuttles rather than walks isn't, wasn't, fair to him?

I don't make the rules, Kurtz! The words I have to describe suspect or unattractive characteristics are themselves suspect or unattractive. When I speak of the scuttling, furtive Kurtz, it will seem to you that I am saying he is the sort of man who, characteristically, scuttles and furts. Who could blame us if we didn't want to meet such a man? Who could blame us if we didn't want to sit in a booth, to crouch in concert, with such a man over his mug or cup or glass? And yet.

Two booths behind us Kurtz crouches with a woman, or without. Together they sit, furtively, speaking perchance of innocent things—though how sinister they seem, stooped.

If Kurtz is furtive, if Kurtz has something to hide—and why should I pretend he is other than he appears?—does that make the woman who is or is not sitting with him "conspiratorial"? Does she keep him company, in their booth, stirring her drink, letting it warm her hands, or else touching it to her face, cheeks smudgy from the heat, to cool her skin in such a manner as to indicate that she is engaged in some abstruse scheme with our dark-haired, dark-eyed, subfusc-sporting Kurtz? They are talking, how can we doubt it, of the myriad unfairnesses visited upon Kurtz since his arrival. If not "myriad," then what? "Many" is more neutral. They are speaking, thinking themselves unheard, of the many ways they might employ to punish us, we who have been so unfair, even in our word choices, to poor Professor Kurtz, so recently come among us, and so unlikely ever to settle.

2.

He hails, I am told, from the east. Sinister, as origins go: night comes sooner there. We offer him a thousand and three belfries and seven railroad stations and still he is nostalgic for the claustral square in the Old Country where no bright electric clocktower lights home the locals to what succor lies in the beds of their crooked-spined wives. Perhaps to be unfurtive in such darkness is to be insolent. Kurtz must descend, you'll agree, from a cautious father and a mother downright stealthy. We might amuse ourselves by imagining the progenitors of Kurtz. To what depths of antiquity could we trace his crouch, his comportment? (Call it *timorous.*) Did they warn him, his clan, not to come among us here in the sun?

I wonder if he's as guarded in speech as in all other aspects of his demeanor. Or if, rather, he's rude, critical, could I say persnickety—which is how I prefer to imagine him. Hard to be guarded when you don't know the customs of your new country, city, workplace. He could think of himself as timid while being brash. Thinking himself droll, he might offend. Imagine my straight-spined wife and I sitting here, in these seats, taking tea with Professor Kurtz! A ridiculous but compelling, what, *Gedankenexperiment.*

I would try, in such a situation, to put our new friend at ease, telling—there's no harm in it—a comical anecdote, a funny story about my college days. For example, the time I climbed up the illuminated clockface in the quad. I would begin, *I was only eighteen at the time—*

But I hate, he'd say, stories that begin with a pronoun. Spare me, please, any more of those awful stories.

What about, I'd ask, humoring him, names, proper names—may I begin a story with a name? Would that meet with your approval, Friend Kurtz? (Thinking: *The nerve!*)

There is no more presumptuous way to begin, he'd say, than with a proper noun. I am willing to bet—and here maybe he'd produce twenty pengő and place them on the table between us—I am willing to bet that you couldn't think of a single name, the syllables of which, pronounced in concert at whatever speed, would not cause me to expire from boredom on this very spot.

Elmer, I'd say, Erich, James, Wendy, Bronislau, Georges, Ludovico, Bernard, Mikis, Dimitri, Franz, Max? (Thinking: *A furtive funeral!*)

You're killing me, he'd confirm.

What about, I'd ask, articles, definite or indefinite, and so forth?

Barely, he'd say, tolerable. Indefinite is almost civilized.

So I should say, I'd say, *An eighteen-year-old boy . . .*

But already, he'd sneeze, you are trying, shamelessly, to get my sympathy for this person. Is that ethical?

This person, I'd say, was *me*, but apparently I'm not allowed to admit it.

It's nothing to be proud of, quoth GedankenKurtz.

So *you* tell a story, I'd suggest.

3.

So little remains, he'd say, of the text from which these details have been drawn. The pages were abandoned, where, in the sun, underwater, between layers of wallpaper. We did all we could to restore them. A few of our staff—overenthusiastic, or else seduced to this or that peculiar partisanship by unscrupulous colleagues—went so far as to attempt to reconstruct the missing text themselves, of course abiding by their own prejudices in so doing. It amazes me what lies they are willing to tell to justify their vandalism. To this day I receive invitations to their symposia, invitations I cannot decline for fear of legitimating their interpretation by dismissing it.

What is clear is that the tablet or manuscript concerns a certain individual. Each time the text is prepared by a new battery of editors and translators for publication in a revised edition, said individual acquires this or that name, these or those characteristics, such-and-such a social class, gender;

his or her pocket or larder is stocked with these or other items the reader might even now find available on sale from this or that vendor. But we will let him or her stand naked, for our purposes, of such craven impedimenta.

The bare individual.

He or she has experiences. (*2 lines unclear . . . unknown no. of lines missing.*)

As a result of these experiences, the individual finds him or herself with different opinions about a certain matter. (*3 lines unclear* . . . the sheep of the queen (?) . . . sheared (?) the wool . . . *7 lines missing or unclear.*)

Even so: this difference proves not so different as he or she had anticipated. (*1 line fragmentary, 6 lines missing, 1 line fragmentary* . . . great mountains . . . *5 lines fragmentary . . . 1 line missing . . . 2 lines fragmentary.*)

Nonetheless, his or her behavior changes as a result. Changes very slightly.

In time, he or she can little remember that he or she had once been other than the way that he or she has become.

The experience that had brought about the initial change seems now to typify the unyielding continuity of his or her life to date. (*The sequence of segments B, C, D, and E, above, is uncertain.*)

To the point that he or she would no longer call it a change, if he or she were here to tell us his or her story in the first person. (*1 line fragmentary* . . . should not find . . .)

To say more than this would be presumption. (*Unknown no. of lines missing.*)

I hope you understand now, Kurtz would conclude.

I understand that you're one cryptic fellow, I'd say. I understand that you aren't going to be much fun at our parties and book launches.

I mean, I hope you understand now why it is that I've been sleeping with your straight-spined wife.

Oh, I'd say, trying to sound worldly. These things happen. (Thinking: *Well, this certainly explains a lot. All that extra time she's been spending in front of the mirror, fixing up her elided correlative comparatives . . . And then, those moods!*)

4.

Why such persecution from this Kurtz, in my bedroom, in my thoughts? Have I done him some material wrong? Have I trespassed on his property? Have I made off with some piece of his property? What offense of mine has Kurtz nurtured in his luxurious hovel until at last he felt it necessary to perpetrate this latest masterpiece upon my unblemished life, vacant of animus these sixty years? Is it my wife he's having coffee with, two booths behind us?

All this, I stress, without our exchanging a single civil word; all this without our trading even the least-sophisticated phoneme—no, not even the guileless */k/*. All this without the muscles of the orbits of his two furtive eyeballs—superior and inferior rectus and perhaps an obscure striated supernumerary, to be cataloged in time by our great doctors—once collaborating in the simultaneous swivel of his chocolate-brown irises to a level approximating my own two candid blues, situated as they usually are thanks to fortune, habit, and breeding nearly a foot and a half above Kurtz's matted tonsure. Without our once standing side by side in the liberal-arts pissoir on the third floor of the St. Cross Building, Manor Road, equipped with workbenches and a piano and floorspace for dance routines and a library of traditional Uzbek wind and rhythm instruments—not least the karnay, kayrok, and koshik. Without our once convincing my straight-spined wife to service us both simultaneously, one of us circumcised and one un-, though don't ask me which is which, using left and right hands, one gloved and one un, probably after imbibing in whatever order suits us out of the three times two times one possibilities available one brandy each from my liquor cabinet to work up the courage for so risky a synod in our little cabin (senior faculty housing, situated conveniently on the campus grounds).

Kurtz would say: You cannot, a priori, perceive me in a way that is not an offense. You, sir, affront the world by recognizing it.

How about I wear tinted glasses, I'd josh.

You do not have the words to find me other than suspect, he'd say.

Nonsense, I'd protest. You're, what, a good guy! A fine chap. How smart you look this morning. This morning your eyebrows are especially bushy, and if their lines on your faces were extended, they would intersect at the point designated *A*, creating four architecturally harmonious though, I fear, incongruent angles. Altogether I would feel quite safe loaning you a sum of money, if such was necessary for you to feed yourself or your many furtive children this coming week, for I have sometimes thought that one of the objects of the Supreme Being in placing what the world calls a weak and unfortunate race in the midst of a seemingly strong and fortunate one is to give the latter the opportunity to continually grow in breadth of thought, in the spirit of tolerance and generosity of purse, by assisting the former. You need only ask, and need only ask once, if you'd like me to come over this very afternoon in my railroad cap and overalls to help you repaper the walls of your home following the unceremonious airing of the original, unbearable flocked pattern of red and green heraldic figures copied from the Hyghalmen Roll by the firm of Ferdinand Barbedienne, and only uncovered due to the recent excavation of that manuscript or tablet, which you now guard so invidiously from your colleagues, once secreted therein by the builder, perhaps, or the original inhabitant, or just some passing conspirator, hoping to hide the most holy book of his or her arcane order, back when our campus was young.

If we have a dean, Kurtz would say, I shall write a letter to him or her about you. You will find yourself traded for one of the hostages still being held by the Department of Hypostatic Abstraction. You'll be lucky if they let you teach ESL to rich Saudi modes of inference next semester.

In fact, I'd persist, I think so highly of our Kurtz that I could at this moment dictate with the utmost sincerity any number of extempore treatises upon his many fine qualities, to wit:

i. On the moderation of Kurtz
ii. On the gentleness of Kurtz
iii. On the shyness of Kurtz
iv. On the dignity of Kurtz
v. On the patience of Kurtz
vi. On the temperance of Kurtz
vii. On the clemency of Kurtz
viii. On the munificence of Kurtz
ix. On the magnificence of Kurtz
x. On the justness of Kurtz
xi. On the prudence of Kurtz
xii. On the foresight of Kurtz
xiii. On the modesty of Kurtz
xiv. On the bravery of Kurtz
xv. On the nobility of Kurtz
xvi. On the religiosity of Kurtz
xvii. On the good conduct and fitting end of Kurtz.

But Kurtz would turn his eyes to the ceiling and protest to his truculent, foreign deity: Do you see how he can't help himself? I walk softly, Kurtz would opine, I avoid working in the office the administration has forced us to share, I eat alone (or with my beloved, straight-spined wife) in the same booth in the cafeteria every day, and I have removed, uncomplaining, my name from our collaborations, even when the work is mine, even when I am myself the subject of the inquiry, even in the seminal study "Abnormalities of Sleep Architecture in Siberian Hamsters and Kurtz" (*Am. J. Sleep Med.*, 2007), wherein my night terrors continue to toil incognito through endless offprints under a revolting alias, and all for the benefit of our great doctors. Really, I am hardly here at all, and still, *still* he must diminish me.

And Kurtz's straight-spined wife, once married to svelte and commendable me, would have no sympathy for her ex—she who still hasn't returned my book of Piranesi reproductions, nor my grandmother's recipe for corn dodgers, and will not answer the phone when Kurtz is away, will not turn on the lights in their cabin, which I can see clear as fingernails from my perch upon the illuminated clock-face in the quad: the minute hand is just wide enough for a lunchbox and thermos of what I will today pretend is Courvoisier.

Me: If anything I've been *too* considerate of you, Kurtz. What haven't I offered you? Doesn't my wife love you more and better and with more substantiating detail than she ever loved me? Are my mattresses not hard enough to support your lower back, ruined from too much slouching? Does my liquor still taste too much of the drugstore where I bought it before pouring it into the cognac bottle I found on the university's pétanque court after your book launch? Haven't I kept an eye on your coffee plantations in Brazil, your apiaries in Aix-en-Provence? Haven't I sprung for a really nice and civil imaginary brunch today, mimosas all around? Aren't you sitting comfortably?

My sciatica is acting up, he'd say. And I'd prefer it if you didn't consider me at all. Look, I'll crouch even lower so as to provide less surface area for the ambient light; I'll scuttle under your chair and back up the wall and into my nest in volume four of your complete Pepys, which your wife was kind enough to bring along when she divorced you.

I know a good chiropractor, I'd say. And then: I'm sorry if that offends you.

Him: I'll feel better as soon as you're thinking about someone else.

And then: Start soon, he'd say. Or steps will be taken.

5.

Word has reached me that the promotion committee has voted—following Kurtz's testimony and that of my ex-wife, as well as a review of the anonymous statements submitted by my few remaining premises, and finally a damning affidavit signed by an old caprice, accusing me of sexual misconduct in the language lab after graduation (while she was still wearing her gown, no less)—to turn down my application to employ the following rhetorical techniques over the coming quarter: peristasis (description of background or circumstances), topographia (description of place or landscape), effictio (complete physical description), chronographia (description of a time or season), pragmatographia (description of a particular narrative or sequence of events), and even anemographia (description of the wind; e.g., what is tousling my wife's hair in that photograph of she and I honeymooning at the temple of Po Klaung Garai, pretending to be Swinhoe's storm petrels engaged in a mating dance). I will be fined for every use of parataxis, though such usages will not in themselves be considered grounds for further censure. One victory: over Kurtz's protests, I have retained free use of catachresis. I hope that you will take my meaning, then, when I say: Kurtz is the unburned ash in my urn. How I'd like to braise the venison of his pulchritude.

Excuse me, but you are on what they call *thin ice*, said someone who might or might not have been Kurtz.

I'm trying, I'm really trying, I might conceivably have considered responding. I get angry sometimes—who wouldn't? But isn't this better? Aren't I improving?

Backsliding, in fact. Gird thy loins, already.

I'm vile, I get it, I abhor myself, I'll stick rags in my mouth—or so I might say in or under such circumstances to someone who was absolutely not Kurtz. You can do anything you want in any way you want and I can't describe it, I'd go on to say. Not even on the sly. Nothing gets past you. I'm not so clever. Who else but Kurtz can be furtive?

Calm down and listen in silence to the breeze you can't describe, unKurtz would council. And don't you dare attribute any more goddamn dialogue to me.

6.

I ask you, is it true that I have so profaned the world in my desire to describe for you the furtiveness of Kurtz? It was begun in all innocence. Now deliberations are underway to have an injunction filed on all of my contingencies by the end of the term. I won't be asked to leave the campus, of course—not openly. But I know I will come in to the office one day to find my last adjectival phrase sitting in the hallway and the locks changed on my noumenon.

What profession am I fit to practice now that the best of me has been eaten by one uncharismatic syllable? What fatal weakness of character tempted me into my first, I thought harmless, speculations on the furtiveness of Kurtz?

I am, it turns out, a monster. How many years had I preyed upon those who could not defend themselves? How many of you have I impoverished with my supposed eloquence? It's a relief to be caught.

So many conversations with Kurtz have been imagined that we need never really speak, yet I still believe that if he would talk to me, give me even a *Gesundheit*, I would be disappointed enough with his real demeanor to find another word for him, another name, and then he could straighten up at last, he could walk like a man, he could take my wife out dancing. I'd get a kick out of that. It would give me hope. But furtive he'll stay, "Kurtz" he'll stay, and I will stay fascinated by this conjunction of sound and sense so long as my worthy colleague continues to take such pains to prevent himself being included in the manuscript or tablet upon which I am now applying my stylus and which I will secret by and by in the walls of my bachelor flat—and so long as he rhymes.

It's nice, however, to sit here with you, eyes down, where first I tried, experimentally, to sketch out a few lines about our new coworker Kurtz, a few booths from Kurtz's accustomed place, where he sits always crouched a few days a week with or without a companion who is probably my wife, and who is, said companion—I am allowed to say so—forlorn, drooping, eroded by my dishonor. They hold napkins, the two of them, in front of their heads, so as to keep their unremarkable faces out of my conversation. The world and my wife.

If they are watching us, furtively, through eyeholes in their paper screens, let us act at least with self-respect, unless I mean *poise*. Shall we raise one last toast together, my friend, before unknown no. of lines missing?

ILLNESS AS METAPHOR

I wasn't happy to hear that my mother had made my diagnosis public. My diagnosis was mine and not hers to publicize. Had I ever publicized her depressions and hunger strikes? Had I ever publicized her flirtations with Rosicrucianism? Had I ever publicized her weakness for amphetamines? Had I ever publicized her six weeks with the White Panthers? Had I ever publicized her mania for the acquisition of Soviet firearms and back issues of *Savage Sword of Conan*? No. Such things are to be kept "in the family." Such things are only for family consumption.

They call now, incessantly, my mother's friends, and ask what my disease is usually called. I can't help them. I can say the name to myself, yes: silently. I can caress its syllables with the intangible tongue I'm still able to wag in my dreams of health. When it comes, however, to forcing the word, wet, into the air, and then through the thirty-six pinpricks in my telephone receiver, I am incapable.

"So you're suffering," they say, my mother's friends.

But to answer them I would need not only to be able to speak about my disease but to be able to put into words sensations that I never bothered, when healthy, to acquire the vocabulary to describe. And now that I'm ill, I am unable to do the research necessary to unearth those words that would best describe to the uninitiated what my illness has done to me.

"But pain," they persist. "Are you in pain?"

I'm certainly not comfortable, I tell them, but am I in pain? They're slow to understand the problem: that in order to speak with clarity about my illness, I would first need to be well; but, being well, it would be impossible to know the first thing about my illness.

They tell me I am being difficult. I say, "It *is* difficult to be ill." They accuse me of wasting their time in order to make a point. I assure them, "There is *no* point to being ill."

"In sum," they say, "you contend that, to speak of your illness, one must, above all, not have contracted your illness."

"That is the dilemma my mother has put us in by speaking out of turn," I tell them. "It was selfish of her to tell you about my diagnosis and so raise your interest in the subject."

"In what sense selfish?" they ask.

"She's concerned about her own reputation," I say. "As a mother. She doesn't like her name to be associated with someone who's never accomplished anything. Anything other than being ill, I mean. She doesn't want to be known as someone who raised a failure."

"The evidence does tend to point in that direction, we admit. The direction of your failure."

I'm not a failure, I tell them. How could I be, when I've succeeded so well in sickness? It's taken decades of work. What might have seemed like indecision to my mother and her friends was, in fact, preparation. What might have seemed like disappointment to them was, in fact, renunciation. What might have seemed to me like tedium was, in fact, discipline.

I've been too disciplined to learn to speak French or to play the violin. I've been too disciplined to finish my correspondence course in copyediting. I've been too disciplined to paint. I've been too disciplined to take a degree in particle physics or molecular pharmacology. I've been too disciplined to move out of my mother's house, too disciplined to marry, too disciplined to contribute to the family finances. All in all, here in my mother's house, between the accumulation of the evidence of my indomitable discipline, and then the evidence left over from my mother's assorted fads, the halls have become enormously difficult to navigate. (If our house is also sick, it's sick with *stuff.*)

My mother stalks me through the piles I've stacked in order to open up a few footpaths through our house full of evidence. We can't seem to agree on which piece of evidence is evidence of what. That violin, I say, pointing, is one of the ones I've shown too much self-control to master. No, my mother rages, I won that at an estate auction last year. Well, I say, I'm in any case quite certain that this pipette here is one of the ones I've shown too much self-control to return to my old lab. Garbage, my mother rails, that's a genuine 1946 Artbeck Pyrex turkey baster I haven't gotten around to cataloguing yet. Well, I say, one thing that brooks no disagreement is that this young man sitting here is one of the ones to whom I've shown too much self-control to volunteer my real name. Not at all, my mother riots, this is Phil, he's just passing through, keep out of his way till his money order comes in.

"The news of my diagnosis ameliorates her failure to make of me anything other than a failure," I explain to her friends. She points me out to visitors, saying, "My daughter is ill." That is my place in the catalogue.

I hear, through the phone, a breath; some ice cubes squeaking into indifferent liquor. A volley of sips. "You're being stubborn," they tell me. "Cut to the chase and tell us what hurts."

"Why court my illness by learning about it?" I ask them.

"Does this mean the illness is communicable?"

"It's incommunicado. Being ill now with my illness, I am unable to make anyone who doesn't have my illness understand the risk they run by doing their feeble best to understand what precisely I can't explain."

"You can't catch a disease over the phone," they scoff.

"To speak about my illness to excess is to risk coming to some sort of understanding of it, and since only people who have my illness can understand it, it stands to reason that understanding in any quantity is dangerous. Even my doctors, being educated women—many of them refugees—were canny enough to question me with caution, by way of much circumlocution, lest an unconsidered word transmit to them if not the proper name than the substance of one of my discomforts, which knowledge would put them too in danger."

"If your own doctors won't discuss your illness with you, what was the gist of their diagnosis?"

"My doctors were unable to say more than that I am suffering conclusively from the illness from which I now suffer. As for myself, I am able to say at the very least that I am unable to say more than the very least."

But my mother's friends have no patience for wordplay. They want data. They want measurable phenomena. They want, for one, to know how much better than me their own children are doing. So now they make remarks implying that my illness sounds more like a social than a physical disorder; to wit, the embarrassment of one's still living, at an advanced age, with one's mother. Upon which I insist that I be allowed to insist that my illness is nothing more than an illness. There is nothing to be said of my illness save that it makes me unwell.

"Then say that," they say. "Say that you're feeling unwell. We're willing to work with generalities. All we ask is that when someone asks after you, we can tell them that you're terrible."

"I don't," I say, "want to mislead you."

"Say a few words about your condition. They don't even have to be the right words, so long as we can agree they refer (if obliquely) to your illness. Maybe we'll be able to progress by analogy?"

"Whenever I try to tell you how I feel, I feel the terminology that would be most apt retreating down a corridor carpeted in heavy orange on a summer night when moisture has caused the flooring to swell and give voice to a bunch of wooden giggles and creaks, which sounds locate in a general way the tread of this errant vocabulary as it staggers off, out of my bed, wearing my slippers, limbs lost in my flannels; but my sonar is not so precise that I can, blindfolded by my illness, reach out with one or both hands to take by the collar this somnambulating lexis before it tips helpless over the balustrade to shriek down to the ill-advised marble parquet installed by my forebears, its head at once buckling into an unrecognizable debutante pink."

"Yes," they say, "that's clear enough, in its way, though this sort of clarity isn't much use."

"I'm not here to be of use to you," I tell them, "but to be ill."

They say that I, so much like my mother, am being selfish. They say that my taking to bed the redheaded baker's boy was pique, not illness. They say that my defacing the Alliance Française was acrimony, not illness. They say that my disrupting those serialist recitals was intolerance, not illness. They say that my expunging their gendered pronouns was hostility, not illness. They say that my appropriating text from the works of Robert E. Howard was indolence, not illness.

"I don't blame you, of course, for these errors," I reassure them. "Misunderstandings are natural, in my condition. There is a gulf between the sick and the well. You'd do better not to lean over it."

"Threats now," they hoot. "So you have nothing more substantial to say, as they say, in your defense?"

"My words are already limping, their straining thews having been pierced by the dagger-points of the desert hordes of my illness, now camped at the Well of Altaku."

"So who needs words," they capitulate. "We'll spare you that effort. Grunt or wail or groan. That would be sufficient."

"As a matter of fact," I tell them, "I'm building you a three-dimensional model of my illness. It's in the garage. It's not finished yet. It will be ten meters by ten meters square, on a raised platform. It will have plaster of Paris hills covered with fuzzy plastic foliage sprinkled on with an implement not unlike a saltshaker, in six realistic colors, standing in for healthy as well as scorched and dying plant life. There will be pipe-cleaner trees and dirt roads made of dirt. There will be a narrow-gauge as well as a funicular railway line. There will be a small town with a single main street. Its cinema marquee will bear little movie titles typed by myself onto decals and applied with fine-point tweezers."

"A mighty undertaking for someone so unwell," they say. "Are you doing all this to spite your mother?"

"My illness explains everything," I say, "but resists explanation. Why not change the subject? How are your own children doing? I trust they're prospering?"

"They're social workers, physicists, brewers, and painters, thanks. None of them are ill. It's not really in their natures. They've never even had colds! They're in the pink."

"That," I say, "is swell."

"But we'll go over your head," they threaten. "We'll talk to your doctors directly. We'll ask if they can't tell us what you've got, in plain English."

"What I've got will get you nowhere. You'd have to get what I've got in order to 'get' it. My doctors get paid to say the same thing. From me you get it for nothing, although not in plain English."

"We haven't gotten a thing. We're phoning your doctors on the other line. They're professionals, we're professionals. We speak the same language. It's a language that doesn't need figures of speech."

"The language of health," I say. Which phrase pleases them.

"And yet I'm rather concerned," I resume, "that you might be ailing."

"We never," they say, confused.

"You sound confused," I say.

"Just tired."

"You sound tired," I say.

"You're trying to turn this around on us."

"I'm trying to turn this around on you."

So they go on the attack: "Are *you* tired? Would *you* call what you're feeling confusion? Why not lie to us, we don't mind it. You know what—give us an adjective and we'll go to bed. That's not too much to ask."

"Concerned is an adjective. Maybe it's a sympathetic illness you've got. Maybe you're sick with sympathy for me."

"Don't kid yourself."

"My mother's oldest friends. Catching their deaths."

"Who's dying?" they ask. "So your illness is fatal?"

"My illness in *you* would be fatal. Me, I'm fine. I've got the strength to be sick. The will. But you, you're not even in the running. You're feeling your age. You should have another drink."

"We're feeling our age," they admit, pouring themselves another drink. "We've been alive a long time. We can even remember you back when you were healthy. How long ago was that? In the playground, giving orders."

"I had ambitions then," I say. "Now I have symptoms. It's not as big a change as it sounds."

"Unless your ambitions *were* symptoms," they snicker. "Snickering symptoms of sickening."

"This is getting serious," I say. "I'm worried that we're beginning to understand one another. You should all definitely see a doctor before it's too late. You'll feel better knowing you tried to save yourselves."

"How is it," they griped, maudlin, "that we none of us have doctors in the family? It would be so convenient."

"The colleges turned your progeny away," I theorize. "The hospitals wouldn't let them intern. They could smell it on them. Susceptibility. Genetic predisposition. Next it'll come for your kids, my illness. Who would have guessed that you were marked for it, all along. I'll admit that I'm surprised. You never seemed the type."

"We're squeamish is all. Too squeamish for doctoring. We don't like the sight of blood. Only the taste, only the sound."

"You're getting worse," I diagnose. "More and more whimsical. *Quick*, a diagnostic test: Describe for me a landscape as seen by an old lady whose disgusting husband just died, but without mentioning the husband or death."

"A landscape," they ponder. "Is it . . . craggy?"

I want to sing *Aha!* Not to mention *Quarantine!* I'd like to step out into the light and do my party piece: Ladies and gentlemen, all you sires and dams of physicists and brewers and social workers! Warn your neighbors, your families, your financial advisers. Tell them to keep their distance, to wear hankies over their mouths. Put up the caution tape, the biohazard signs, fence yourselves in. Your houses are plague nests, just like my mother's. Your kitchens and corridors will run beige with dust and discipline. You'll lose definition, and when you're gone—it won't take long!—I'll do you the favor of tending your graves, and I'll always retain the self-control to neither dance nor piss upon your private soil. In the end, when I've followed you, no hops will be planted over us. The land will lie fallow for seventeen generations. You're my mother's friends, but—after all—my mother is the mother of plague. You ought to have known to mind your own business. You don't appease illness by containing it. You appease it by spreading it.

But no, instead I say, "You'd better come along with me to my next checkup."

"May we?" my mother's friends ask, cowed. "And where do you go, with no job, and no money? A charity ward? What's it like?"

“Rude jests fly back and forth,” I tell them, “as the patients gnaw beef and thrust their muzzles deep into jugs of ale.”

“That’s *exactly* how we imagined it,” they say.

HENRIETTA THE SPIDER

Archibald's sister lived in the addition, past the far bedroom wall, but her snoring came through as though there were no wall at all, and Archibald's wife Henrietta listened to it every night, her hand on what she'd call her mons pubis, above her gown, just covering it, cupping it, not even applying pressure, but good and ready to do so should Archibald stop turning, punching his pillows, the bed quaking on its casters, which state of affairs lasted until the sun rose and the traffic noise started, and he finally slept and his sister was drowned out, and Henrietta got up to start breakfast, so tired she put the sugar in the fridge, so tired she fried an orange peel once and started a fire. That's when Archibald had asked what was wrong—it had taken a fire—but there was no use chatting about it. Henrietta found life irreducible. Talking didn't break it up or make it go down easier. If Archibald ever raised his hand to her in anger—which he never had, of course—but *if* he did, or if she happened to kill their dog—Archibald and his sister's, that golden puppy, that soulful-eyed pup, as she had often thought of doing, the serrated bread knife in the mound of its belly or in the ruff of its neck, so furry there you could miss the skin completely if you weren't careful—then those actions, regrettable though they'd be, could never be made bite-size by complaining about them; they would always be there, in her memory, like outposts in the desert, with no moisture in the air to make them rot.

As a result, Henrietta tried to effect as little as possible. Archibald and his sister didn't understand. The woman would would leave a shoe in the hall, in from the snow, melting, spoiling the rug, or else Archibald would speak harshly to Henrietta—not because he was angry at her, but because of other worries, work-worries—then forget about it, forget it had ever happened, and neither he nor his sister would realize that they had altered Henrietta's conception of them permanently; that she carried these slights with her everywhere, and that they came up out of the sand when she took her baths, peevish, speculating on the color of Archibald's sister's pubic hair. It would be the same color as their dog, of course, and perhaps as soft to the touch. You could miss the heat and blood underneath if you weren't sure it was there.

Henrietta was large, she was large all over, she had large feet and large thighs and large breasts, matronly breasts, and she knew she looked like a mother; her body was a mother's body, although she and Archibald were childless. Archibald's sister was flat-chested, skinny, like Archibald himself had been twenty years before, and Henrietta loved it, her skinniness, her impossible skinniness, like an animal's. Where had she read that fat people, large people—because they were so corporeal, so much taken up with their skin and organs, all out of proportion to their bones and nerves—were indolent, inertial by nature, only concerned with their own comfort; while skinny people, their flesh so restrained, were free to be cerebral, to accomplish things, to be extroverted and involved with the world. Archibald's sister was quick and nervous. She didn't like to sit. She spent every day out of the house, only coming back after dark. Henrietta didn't know what she did out there. She didn't even know if Archibald's sister had a job; Archibald bought the food and didn't make the woman pay rent. Though Henrietta read all of Archibald's sister's mail, and often went into the addition during the day to poke around, she knew as little now about Archibald's sister as when the woman had first moved in. At the time, Henrietta had been sure that it would kill her. She foresaw strange men coming into her house to stay the night, leaving their gray messes on Henrietta's clean sheets and Archibald's sister's legs and stomach, like slugs parading over virgin leaf. But there were never any men—Henrietta was quite sure of this—and here they were, the three of them, so many years later, and everything was just the same, Henrietta still feeling as though she would die any day now, just shrivel in her fat inertia from wanting so much to tiptoe over to Archibald's sister during the night and put bites into her tiny, taut shoulder tendons.

It was in the bath, after making herself come, that she noticed the marks, ten ugly dots on her side, with blue and purple and paper-white lines like twigs or sparks emerging from each: colors she hadn't known her body could make. She poked them and they didn't hurt. She squeezed them and they didn't burst. She spent most of that day pacing because of them and so didn't have dinner ready in time, which made Archibald irritable, and Archibald's sister slip away so politely that Henrietta started to cry. Archibald—the sweetheart—desisted at once, though the crying had nothing to do with him: politeness was so brilliant to Henrietta that she couldn't bear to look at it directly. By bedtime she was running a fever, and she began to dress in the bathroom to keep Archibald from seeing the marks.

She slept that night, so deeply that she didn't notice Archibald fix his own breakfast or leave to give his sister a ride into town. She woke up panicked, with a terrible headache, disoriented and slow. She went into the kitchen to make herself coffee and saw that the dog was lying in front of the fridge, a pond of fur: dead, obviously dead, not moving or breathing, its limp tongue an islet, pink amid blond. They always kill the dog first, in horror movies, she thought. It's lazy. It's cruel. Henrietta was determined not to dignify the event with screaming. But, then, she was positive that she was responsible, and screaming would only call attention to her crime. Yes, she had killed the dog, maybe in her sleep, and how was she going to live it down? She walked over the to body and knelt in her nightdress to touch the dog's neck, where she knew she would have cut it. Her hand disappeared up to the wrist, sinking into the dog's softness, and when she did find the skin, she was surprised to feel it still warm and pulsing. She took her hand out and felt a tickle, saw that an unassuming brown spider was clinging to it, riding her hand out of the dog's fur into the open air. The spider was so small Henrietta almost missed it; it dropped magically, even courteously to the floor before she could be frightened, and disappeared into the carpet.

The dog made a noise now, a disgusting noise, both a wheeze and a belch, and this was worse than its being dead, because Henrietta knew that she would have to do something. The dog groaned and Henrietta was sure that it would void its bowels or something equally dreadful if she didn't get it out of there right away. She looked through Archibald's desk until she found a receipt from the vet and called the number on it.

They sent a car, an old station wagon with bad shocks and a red blanket for the dog to lie on, and Henrietta had to squeeze herself in back next to it, because the passenger seat was taken up by the cage of an animal she never got a good look at, though it made adding-machine noises all through the ride. She watched the dog breathe like a swell of dry grass and hated it and imagined she could smell its rot. Only when they reached the clinic and she got out, woozy, did she think to herself: an ambulance for animals, fancy that! They brought out a tiny stretcher and took the dog inside. Henrietta waited in the waiting room and read magazine articles about Lyme disease and Mozart. When the vet came out to see her, he touched her hand, and she hated him for it. "You're like ice," he said, frowning. This instead of comforting her.

He went back into his office and came out with a thermometer. It looked too big to have been made with a human in mind. Arguing with him in front of the other people in the waiting room would be more humiliating than giving in. It read one hundred and two.

"You should be in bed," the vet said. Henrietta reminded him about the dog, crossing her fingers in her pocket and hoping the animal was good and dead. It was.

"We found bites," the vet told her. "Like volcanoes." He held up his hands palms out and shook his head. He didn't say more. He gave her two aspirins from his secretary's desk and told her to get a lot of rest. When Archibald came later to collect her, the vet talked to him about getting the house sprayed, and Henrietta stole twenty or so of the thick waiting-room magazines on her way out, holding them in front of her, blocking the sight of them with her body. Though she'd hated the dog, she felt that its death entitled her to consolation by whatever means took her fancy. She was queasy in the car, and the slick magazines slid off her lap and onto the rubber mat at her feet, where they got soaked.

Archibald carried them in, surprised at Henrietta's insistence, then went back for his wife, who felt too sick to walk alone. She slept fourteen hours and dreamed of Archibald's sister. She came into the bathroom where Henrietta was taking her bath. She kneeled by the bath. She made herself accessible. Henrietta was in such a hurry to get up and do something—maybe embarrass them both by shrieking for Archibald—that she hit the woman's little face with an elbow, bloodying Archibald's sister's nose and bruising one of her eyeballs, which turned purple and wet. The house was empty when Henrietta woke, and the magazines were stacked on a chair in the dining room. Instead of making coffee, she sat down and took one and opened it on the coffee table, though its edges were curled and the paper rippled like the skin on old milk. There were photographs of a regular spider's web, and then of webs that were markedly different, made by spiders in a research lab who had been given a variety of drugs, like mescaline or caffeine. The article described the spiders as little machines, that's all: web-making automatons that made no decisions. The blueprints for the structures they built were inherited, genetic. The drugs changed these patterns without the spiders being aware. Their webs became ornate, or else haphazard and aimless. Either way, inefficient.

Archibald came home early that day, surprising Henrietta in the bath. She pulled a towel off the rack and sat down again, wrapping it around her in the water to cover the marks, and its edges floated.

"I thought you'd gone out," Archibald said, and retreated. Henrietta wondered where he thought she would have gone. "Is there something the matter with your arm?"

She got out of the bath and put on her clothes. The marks felt brittle and conical under her shirt, like little buildings. The towel she left in the tub, and it sluiced toward the drain when she let the water out, blocking it.

Archibald cooked dinner again that night but Henrietta didn't eat. She hid in their room until he and his sister went to bed, then came out and made coffee. She wasn't tired anyway. She read the rest of the magazines and threw them out. She was very careful to be quiet.

On her hands and knees in front of the fridge she pushed down the piles of the carpet; between them like scalp ran a strange texture, sandy and rubbery, printed with what felt like a grid. She was looking for that spider, but of course it would have heard her coming; it would be under the fridge or up on a wall; she could even be killing it right now, one of her knees pressing it down and crushing it dead.

Someone rang the bell the next day. Henrietta woke up terrified and looked out the peephole. She saw an exterminator, shut off the lights and sat against the door until he went away. When she'd calmed down she went and pushed the fridge away from the wall but saw nothing behind it but rolls of dust. She was too tired to move it back afterward and resigned herself to asking Archibald for help when he got home.

She checked all the closets and under the beds, as well as between the mattresses and the box springs. She put on her robe and a jacket and went down to the garage—but wouldn't it be too cold for them there? The floor was concrete and cluttered with pebbles and Henrietta could see her breath. She thought, shivering: nothing can live down here. There were terrible noises as the electric door went up and Archibald pulled in, his sister in the passenger seat. Henrietta ran back upstairs as quickly as she could; in the headlights she knew anyone on the sidewalk or across the street could have seen her, her legs showing, barefoot. She hadn't even had her bath yet. She went into the water right away, little rocks coming off her feet when she submerged them, and she ignored it when Archibald or his sister knocked on the door and even tested the knob, which of course she had remembered to lock. It came to her while she was soaking that the boiler was in the garage, and that the hot water came up through the floor from there—the spiders could have nested near the pipes. She double-checked when Archibald and his sister were asleep and found some cobwebs there but nothing more. Had they moved on?

The only place left to look was the attic. It wasn't a proper attic, with boxes and yellowing blinds, but more of a crawlspace, never explored, that extended over the master bedroom. Henrietta took a sturdy chair out of Archibald's sister's room and put it below the hatch; the panel moved up easily, and she peeked her head up into the dim light. By the tickling she felt on her scalp and cheeks, she knew she had found them. She pulled herself all the way in. They were keeping their distance; Henrietta had ripped away a wide swatch of web by her entrance and now they were frightened, or else too gracious to acknowledge her gaffe. She sat for what she supposed was an hour, dizzy with her fever, but they wouldn't come nearer, even after she held out her arm to one, hoping to encourage it to swing down on a thread and greet her, to climb aboard; even after she fell asleep, expecting to wake up covered in their zigs and zags, the spiders drinking her blood and making new awkward webs because of its influence. No: they hung, tiny fruit, and ignored her. It was frustrating.

At last she gave up and went back to the hatch. She would have to find a way to entice them. Now she could hear that Archibald and his sister had come home and started dinner. They had put the sturdy chair back where it belonged, so Henrietta called them to help her down. She was surprised when they didn't ask her any questions. She called a cab and found a pet store the next afternoon and came home with a large white puppy. She'd left a note on the door to keep the exterminator away while she was out. It said "We don't need you."

The dog was gentle and four feet long and took to her at once. It made a show of familiarizing itself with the house when she let it in, looking at her for approval, or just to make sure that she saw it was pleased. Archibald and his sister went wild for it: Archibald forgot to be anxious for Henrietta and played with the thing, slapping its seedpod belly and throwing it things to fetch, though it didn't understand what he intended. His sister's response was tender and restrained, more of a quiet appreciation, an admiration from afar, which was as wild a look from her as Henrietta ever saw.

She was a little put off by their readiness to accept this new complication into their home—they had seemed so attached to the old dog—but Henrietta could see that the animal she'd chosen was a great improvement on the last. It was demure, or as demure as a dog can be, and knew how to make itself scarce. It came when you called, despite not having a name, and looked at you with a kind of intelligence, or at least curiosity, whereas the dead dog had been dim to the end. It probably hadn't even known it was dying when it lay down that morning in front of the fridge, despite what people say about animals having a sense for these things.

Henrietta could see that Archibald and his sister were relieved. They thanked her for what they considered a gift and Archibald forgot to take Henrietta's temperature that night before he went to bed. She only got to sleep when they'd left for the day and then woke up early and got out the sturdy chair to put underneath the attic hatch. She took the new dog into her arms and popped it through, but it wasn't long before the bewildered pooch leapt down again, upsetting Henrietta and her chair and landing all three of them on the floor. Hurt, Henrietta said something aloud she couldn't later recall. The next time she made sure to close the panel before the white dog could think to jump. She heard it sit down and was thankful it was so calm and well behaved. She'd take her bath and then check on it later. In the tub, she saw that the marks on her side had all but disappeared.

In her robe, with her hair up, Henrietta retrieved the dog from the attic. She was surprised but pleased to see that it was still alive; for one thing, this made it easier to carry to the bathroom. The dog was eager to be comforted, and didn't seem to blame Henrietta for what she'd done. She put it down into the tub, mostly dry now, and forced it to sit by pressing on its rump; its fur soon sopped up the last holdout domes of soapy water from her soak. She took

Archibald's sister's comb from the cabinet and looked for spiders on the animal, ridging back its coat like a gardener. They were easy to find in his whiteness, and the bites were indeed like volcanoes, more horrible than her own had been, like something dreadful and subterranean in the new dog's skin that the attackers had just teased to the surface. Her head was splitting by the time she called it quits, with twenty of her tenants—varying in size, though uniform in their markings and color—lowered on a longer tine of Archibald's sister's comb into a clear plastic container and covered before they could crawl away.

She patted the dog's head and left it to convalesce or expire. She would let the spiders loose on her and Archibald's sister's bed linen. Henrietta hadn't counted on this being a chore, but it was just as difficult to coax the creatures out of their corral, one at a time, as it had been forcing them in; ten each would do, she figured: three at the headboard, three at the foot, four in the center—still using the comb. Sometimes a crowd of five or six would scurry out when the lid was cracked, and Henrietta was forced to recapture these truants by hand, hoping she wasn't causing them pain. What was it like, she wondered on their behalf, to be handled by something so enormous that it couldn't even imagine your distress? All the electricity of their nerves and brains couldn't even light an itch up my leg, she thought. And yet she felt that she and they had come to an understanding.

It took them a few minutes to disperse on the bed she shared with Archibald, because of its size. On his sister's twin, though, they disappeared faster than Henrietta could follow. Her work had exhausted her. She lay down on the couch, feeling sluggish and scrambled, imagining the bugs sinking down into the family sheets and blankets like salt in soup. She fell asleep, comfortable and hot, even out in the open, where Archibald and his sister would probably come across her and wonder and worry at her behavior; maybe ask her again to see a doctor, maybe make another appointment she would forget.

It could be, she thought, that her fever was going down, and this likelihood left her with a feeling of loss. The white dog came out of the bathroom and lay down on the floor in front of her.

That night she made sure to go to bed at the same time as Archibald and his sister, hoping maybe to catch the spiders at their work, crawling over her husband, biting his neck or cheeks or forehead; simply, without fanfare, certain they could digest him. Archibald was relieved and made love to her for the first time in months; Henrietta, thinking of his sister, hoped that she could hear it through the wall, and that maybe it turned her stomach—that Henrietta could be like a bug in her stomach. The dog, still breathing, forgetful and forgiving, took to sleeping outside their door. Archibald joked after a few days of this that the animal must *enjoy* their tripping over it in the night, on the way to the bathroom or again in the morning, when the alarm went off and Henrietta got up to make breakfast, having listened to its breathing and the impact of its tail flopping against the jamb for seven hours running.

While she waited at night, without hope, for the dog or Archibald to fall sleep, or for the spiders to finally make their appearance, the days of her sickness recurred in her memory and vied now with Archibald's sister's face and body for precedence in her thoughts. She had *done* something, she knew: somehow focused herself and done something permanent and inexcusable. Something that should, now, like a new piece of furniture, be a lasting obstacle in the house: something to be maneuvered around in the night. But there was no change—or none that she could see. The exterminator never came back, and Henrietta fell asleep on her feet during the short funeral ceremony Archibald and his sister performed for their old dog; her grip on the new one's leash firm as she dozed and it tried happily to break loose and dig. Neither Archibald nor his sister ever fell ill and neither mentioned Henrietta's spell. The spiders had betrayed her and fled, she knew, and still Archibald loved her, his sister never complained, and the white dog was game for anything. A nightmare.

It was weeks then before Henrietta felt an itch on her side while she sat luxuriating in her bath. She scratched there at the site of her old wound, just above the water, and felt a mass of tiny, fragile foreign bodies rather than skin. She wouldn't look or move and so the water went cold on her. When Archibald came home he knocked and knocked. His sister needed to pee.

THE KNACK OF DOING

This is the story, he says, unclean thing, abomination of desolation, spitting a little into the mouthpiece. He was thinking, he says to his once-wife, that he, of the two of them, is the angrier: the medal goes to him, his anger is like unto the sun in its endless fizzle. His anger is on the table, she should weigh, she should measure, she can imagine it as a sort of a demipenteract; which by the way is a five-dimensional hypercube, whereas her complaints are, as it were, strictly 2D. She should, he says, *go* and *do*, and then come and tell him back whether this anger of his is now in fact, as he suspects, a greater anger than her own, being more complex, better realized, more substantial.

But back she tymbals on the earpiece with she can't come to the phone right now, so please leave your name, number, and a brief message.

And he says, harlot, hemistich, how subtle thou art, what he's hearing you say is that you are so furious with him, that your anger is so much *angrier* than his, that you have become wholly rigid, you can hardly move, you are the petrified woman, you recline on a slab, unable to croak out more than these few words, which hardly sound as though they're issuing from a human being with a body temperature of ninety-eight point six degrees Fahrenheit, though he remembers now that you actually tended to run a little hot, which he found he guesses appealing, he's able to admit that now.

And she says back, she's sorry, but the number you have reached is no longer in service.

And he says, jezebel, midden, catastrophe, again you best him, again he's cut down, you outclass him every step of the way; your command of their common language shows him up as pinchbeck and poetaster, here you are giving him the supreme metaphor, the image of images, you're so furious, he says, so incensed, that you are effaced entirely, you are *not at home*, there is no home, you have immolated yourself in your anger. Who is he to compare his meager discontent to this supreme rage? You are the last word in anger, my darling, my dimmerswitch. He is shamed, he is beaten, he is defeated—he isn't even angry anymore, you know what, he's actually feeling a little better, he admires you, he wor-ships you, he's sorry he ever got in the ring with the champ.

But that was when, he can't even find the phone these days, and months is as good an estimate as any, months and months since last they shared a bed, he means carnally, he means the meat-bed of marriage. The jinx started, he says, with his grandiloquent granduncle. They had never been close, he'd seen the guy once or twice on holidays, found him a bit unnerving, too tall, too skinny, too spooky, too little interested in anyone else's opinions, too intent on calling his grandnephew's comics, which the boy had hauled around with him even to the dinner table, even to synagogue, "them funny books." The men in the family tended toward roundness, but not this one. They tended toward bonhomie and puns, but this granduncle was a haunting. He memento mori'd even children's birthday parties. All he could talk about was the Hitler War, the Hitler War had had made him a machine fit only to talk about the Hitler War. Whatever you said to him he could turn back onto the Hitler War; you hadn't even known you were *already* talking about the Hitler War until he backed you into the corner. He wasn't invited to weddings, as a rule. Three years, he said, in a cowshed. Three years eating bugs and rats. What else is there to talk about?

When they came for me there was two of them, Germans, he said. They took me out into the woods. There was a particular tree they liked to water with blood. That's some heavy Norse shit, said his then-teenage nephew. One stayed in the car, one walked me out into the forest, the uncle went on. Is a forest the same thing as a wood? asked his nephew. What they didn't know is that I had a knife in my boot; I always had a knife in my boot, said the uncle. You killed him? his nephew asked, interested now, and yes, he for sure killed him, and that's why he lived, at least till he died. He came to the States, never married, lived with one of his sisters in a city I can't much care about. Maybe Wilmington, Delaware?

So the uncle calls and asks will his grandnephew edit his memoirs—his awful, really just unbearable memoirs about his unbearable experiences. And he sends them over, in a box, one of those manila folder boxes that ought to be outlawed on account of how many maniacs keep their manuscripts in them. And he sends some money, the uncle, which his nephew can surely use, since he's still supporting his son on and off, his son who's working as a cabbie now; he quit school, is just screwing around, really screwing around, screwing around as much as possible; apparently cabbies can really clean up, as it were, nookiewise, bringing women home in the wee hours, particularly if you happen to forget about the fare. And he, the father, was made to hear about every one of these adventures, every item in each week's pornographic inventory; his then-wife was exempt, it was guy talk, who knows where the kid got his ideas, he thought maybe there would be a natural sort of interest shared between them, but it was the first time they'd ever even mentioned genitalia in each other's presence since the boy was about three.

A year, more, in this fashion; the uncle's manuscript grew a white beard, and aside from a bit of anxiety whenever our putative editor reached for a paperclip or pencil and felt the hairs on whichever wrist was closest to its evil hum on his desk try to yank themselves electrically out of their sockets, he didn't really spare a thought for the job he'd agreed to do: just took his granduncle's money and ran, if by running you mean sitting still.

I'm a bad person, he told his wife one day. Not at all, she said; a bad person would have just told his granduncle to go to hell, or said "I'm busy": you're more like a war criminal. I'm not hurting anyone, really, he said, hurt. Next morning came a call from his own father, the granduncle's actual and ungrand nephew: the old man had had a stroke. Had the uncle made it? He hadn't made it. The funeral would be next-next morning; would the grandnephew be able to make it? But no, he made it only as far as the bus station. Someone pushed him, some woman it looked like, shoved him probably without malice when he was just about to essay the fatal final tin-plated step between sidewalk and bus aisle; he tripped and fell forward and smacked his face against the metal runnels in the second of the bus's three TV-tray-sized stairs. It's a whammy! he announced to his wife after Hatzalah drove him home, face wrapped in gauze, led into the foyer by two restless paramedics: a curse! Both his retinas had detached, and permanent or not, being struck blind is being struck blind—it's hard not to take it personally, which is to say biblically. The prospect of never again seeing December bleach a ladybug, never again laying eyes on Goudy Old Style or Hanna Schygulla! Divine retribution, he called it, unless it was only the cumulative effect of decades of really expert onanism now hitting him all at once (oh, the tyranny of proficiency!). No, no, it was no accident, it was his uncle, could only be his bitter grand-damnuncle putting in a word with the Blessed is He, hexing his nephew from beyond the grave, and all on account of his putative editor's terrible behavior with regard to that terrible memoir! Why should I have to suffer for my uncle's suffering, he asked his wife—shouldn't it be enough that *he* suffered for it? And, anyway, honey, why didn't you come get me at the hospital? Nobody's home, commented the ambulance driver. Look, said his passenger, I'm not crazy, I'm just going to be blind for a bit—keep your remarks to yourself. I mean the house is empty, said the driver, for real: there's no one here but us three. Though *also*, said the second EMT, you're probably crazy?

He's still in the dark today, in the dark about the whereabouts of his wife and his phone and his son, his son who'd volunteered, for a time, right after the accident, to buy his groceries for him, his son the cabbie who from time to time came by, who came out of his way, out of his way from time to time out of filial devotion, up over the Tappan Zee to leave milk and butter and make coffee and talk about, well, *brag* about, well, just think, just think how many times their son the cabbie must have scored since his father went eremite, blind and celibate, the tally must be enormous, he himself in the dark having never made it out of the single digits, in all frankness, married as he was at the acme of his failure to compete with his coevals with respect to pussy, which leads him to think, sure, bear with me, of his uncle's manuscript, source of his woe, lost somewhere on the disaster of his desk: those two SS men, of course in long black leather coats and peaked hats, finding his granduncle in his hiding place and driving him in their big black car out into the big black woods to do him dirty—which always struck him, you know, as being a little out of their way, what the point was of this it's hard to say, surely you didn't need to head out of town to kill a Jew in them days—yet somehow they'd forgotten to search him before they motored out into the ink with this armed and dangerous Yid: sporting, unbeknown or knownst to them, a leather knife in his left boot. One German waits in the car singing from *Tannhäuser* and the other one marches uncle through the trees to execute him maybe far enough away that his sensitive, music-loving partner won't have to scrape brains off his glasses again this week, how many times is too many do you think. Uncle stabs the SS man and takes off into the woods, he makes himself scarce, he survives, and here's the connection: comparing each of these as they're called real-life situations—Junior the cabbie Casanova on the one hand, uncle on the other—is there a moment, could you isolate a second or yocto- or zeptosecond in either of these cases, either of these cases where quick thinking and resolve and all sorts of other boy-scout qualities come into play that the father alone in his home in the dark is lacking altogether, is there a moment, he asks, an identifiable *particule* of time in which you could say that one's hopes or plans for direct action thaw out and puddle into certainty?

He can't tell, he has no one to ask, if he's come unmoored from what you could call common human experience—has he, always so passive, procrastinatory, become such a lump at this stage in his decline that he can't actually remember what it is to initiate and then carry through an action? But no, here's proof that he still acts in and upon the world: he moves, he plots himself a course in the mornings from his bed through the forest of bumps, stubbings, scratches, and thwacks to his desk or to the fridge or to the front door to feel the wind on his, well, everything, he hasn't bothered to put more than a bathrobe on in days now, or indeed to the toilet (or what, he jokes to himself, he sure *hopes* is the toilet, tee and then hee)—so even in his current confusion he's still no stranger to causality, to action, to *accomplishment* (getting around is an accomplishment). What he can't savvy is the decision to stab or fuck someone becoming the act of fucking or stabbing—is it already a reality in the deciding or planning, or is there a moment when the event, the tangible event could still be averted, could go awry, the knife slipping, the partner unwilling, *enfin*, to engage in such a transaction? If the former, could one say his son has always and will always fuck such and such a woman in return for or as a result of or even despite his giving her a free ride home drunk from the club or bar in which, perhaps, for god's sake preserve the species, she was looking to be fucked? And, likewise, could one say that his son's great-great uncle was never in any danger, that night, from the two SS men, or at least the one who was going to shoot him, because he had already and always decided that he, uncle, would kill him, Horst, first? Or does your intent require a willing or anyway persuadable object, a person wanting to get fucked, a Nazi wanting to get stabbed? Because, okay, brass tacks: *he*, the father of the fucker, the grandnephew of the stabber, would never have been able, in their positions, to pull off what it is they pulled off.

In a cab working the cold early mornings, driving people home drunk from clubs or bars, he'd get about as much action as here in the dark in the dust. In the woods with a pointy SS man he would, what, hope the guy might have a change of heart? Even with a knife in his boot, and he can imagine *this* very clearly, maybe he's dreamed it, that pressure on his ankle bone, though what kind of boot would it have been, probably pretty high on the calf, not cowboy boots but what would you call them (period detail is important)—even with that knife in his boot he probably would try (is this what they call the death instinct?) to talk himself out of fighting for his own life, would have told himself you don't have a chance, why even bother, you're kidding yourself that you could crouch down and get that knife out without Hans here noticing what you're doing; knowing your luck it's probably wedged in there pretty good, what a laugh, maybe the fellow with the gun'll be polite and wait for you to pry the thing out: fair's fair, Fritz. And say he managed it after all, okay, he gets the knife out and sticks it, where, in Werner's body; even say he sticks it in precisely the right place the first time out and the Nazi crumbles—that's the word, cookies and corpses crumble, what a paradise is English!—to the forest floor, covered with fir needles, do firs have needles, bleeding onto the pricks of green, add some snow, the pricks of green in the white-dusted . . . enough, the man bleeds to death in a trice, a needle-bleeding-prick-blood trice, he rolls over and when he stops his black coat slivered green and dirty gray looks in the dark like a sudden thaw, leaving you, where? In the woods or forest with no food, no way to get any, miles from town, another German waiting in a car with another gun that will kill you just as dead back on the road, his machine at simmer, listening to *Your Nazi Hit Parade*, feet cold, but not so cold as yours, you huddled in the snow, waiting for the sun to rise, the sun that will only make you a bigger target . . . for *this* you fight for your life?

Is it that it skips a generation? He means this knack of *doing*. His uncle and now his son are or were, what, in the thick of life, the marrow or whatever, they decide and their decisions have consequences, they are *agents*, they *act*, they *effect*. Or: the species, the culture, it acts through them—they are in concert with what is basic in the animal, while he, in *his* neck of the woods, at his desk, in the dark . . . he is the chaff, he is what's discarded, cut out, boiled away; already he's overripe. If this nation were truly strong et cetera it would not tolerate the likes of him: unfit, unproductive, unwell, unbearable, uninterested; a scoundrel, parasite, swindler, profiteer.

As an experiment though he takes a detour and finds, you know what, it's easy to imagine himself as the *object* in each of these scenarios (stabbing/fucking)—what clarity results!

He's tuned to the right channel! In the cab he could be the husband, say—well, it had more or less happened, late at night, tired and drunk, with his wife flirting or whatever she did with the driver, not her own son in actual fact but same age difference, the ratios are the same though the contents differ—and suddenly it's more an *of course* they go to bed with him, these women: the trick is not to leave out the observer. Otherwise, look, talking a strange woman into bed occupies a superposition, she is willing and reticent, awake and passed out, everywhere at once, you're fucking her in the back seat, in her apartment, at the doorman's station, in an alley, on a tarpapered rooftop or lead-paint fire escape, her mother's bed, her kid's room—but no, put yourself into the scenario and it all snaps into place, there is one cabbie and one woman and one husband who's nodding off but listening nonetheless to their patter.

When she was a little girl, he imagines her saying, because she was one once, a little girl, we have pictures, photographic evidence, when she was a little girl her uncle took her out into the woods, it was November, or maybe December, anyway it was the end of the year, the end of a year of her little girlhood, the family was out vacationing in the plains, they owned a little, what, freehold? and it was close to the end of their time there, she says, and it was the end, she says, of her little girlhood, sure, draw a line under that motherfucker, and there among the fir needles her uncle, well, you probably know where this is going, and ever since then, she says, she can't help but feel that there's a violence, you know, in the act, what she probably would call the *brute* act, or, more to the point, the sex isn't about the sex, it's, how did she put it, "an exchange of power," that's where the money is, folks.

And the cabbie's like, look, you want he should take FDR or Second? But the husband knows, the father knows, his forehead smeared against the glass of the passenger window, buttering the pan, looking, if his eyes are open, down and back to where her dress pouts forward over her boy's chest, he just *knows* this kid, young enough to be their son, is flirting back, though you'd need an instrument as sensitive as how-many-years'-worth of watching her at work to pick up the signal. The jerk is completely taken in, Christ, he's never even *considered* that the fucking/stabbing binary might not be oppositional but unitary, holy hopping shit, lady: when he gives it to his girlfriend this weekend he's sure as hell going to have a different perspective!

And then the knife, there too it makes perfect sense to him if he puts himself in the stabbee's place. Someone decides, sorry, it's him or you buddy, and so takes out a tool with which he can abridge your life. Impossible for this man in the dark in the dirt to imagine making the decision to end someone else's life, but to imagine someone else ending *his*, that comes as easily as the moon. Back among the firs the uncle and his witchy niece watching him, everyone washed in the colors of the coffee ring the blind man can stickily feel and remember the sight of on his right-hand armrest, where, mornings, he used to rest his reckless mug; burned the fuck out of his upper thigh when once a little spilled, but concentrate: the three, under the bright brown moon, a standoff, isosceles—he, the father, has a gun; he, the uncle, has a knife; she, the niece, has a secret. We're gonna have a real good time together.

IV.

DELETE THE MARQUIS

1. It was only as I stepped down from the rickety diligence that had brought us the greater part of the distance to that lonely place at the cartographical (though indiscernible) partition between the *départements* of Tarn-et-Garonne and Gers—our unenthusiastic driver helping to transfer first the luggage and then the persons of his two remaining passengers, myself included, to the less commodious if more discreet milieu of the vis-à-vis sent ahead from the estate to which we were bound, a conveyance found waiting, its own driver sitting and smoking a few paces distant, in the dust of the road outside of a small town whose name I can no longer recall—that I was forced into an initially somnolent and thereafter acutely anxious recognition of the fact that this last holdout among my traveling companions of the past several days had not only been bound all the while for the same destination as myself, but was known to me from my youth, and therefore on both counts posed a distinct threat to my aim of maintaining an absolute incognito on this delicate expedition.

2. That the man might also be seeking treatment from the famed Amand-Marie-Jacques de Chastenet, Marquis de Puységur, was in itself no great worry (I would, I told

myself, insist on private and discreet consultations with the Master, and if the Marquis refused this requirement, I would sneak away to the nearest town, on foot if necessary, foolish though this would make me feel), but his familiarity to me was, on the other hand, a matter of no small astonishment, not to mention dreadful consternation, since this perfumed individual had when we were both children been a servant known to hail from a family of no means; Victor was taken in to wait upon my father during the last days of that debauched malingerer's first and final proper illness, and though the boy had been a devoted enough employee, his seeming transformation into the foppish thing now facing me flew in the face of every rational conjecture I might have harbored about the fate of that luckless child—might have harbored, I mean to say, if I'd ever spared little Victor a single thought in the intervening years—if only on account of his prodigious stutter, listing eye, and profound vagueness of mind; and yet I doubted that even a simpleton such as the boy I remembered from my father's chambers could fail to recognize the first-born son and heir of his not especially lamented master here in the wide light of midday and at such close quarters as these: a recognition that would have been pungently uncongenial even under ordinary circumstances, let alone embarked as I was upon an errand the nature of which I did not care to see publicized.

3. Having given him no more than a disinterested fellow traveler's oblique appraisal till the moment we changed

carriages—he had been seated to my left and had spent most of our riding time asleep with his hat over his eyes; or else, during those few hours he was waking, hunched in a scribbling frenzy, scratching with futile industry in pen and ink on the rectos of a daybook already so blackened by extant notes as to resemble an amateur landscapist's attempt at anatomizing a blank black wall of onyx or a moonless winter fog—I had decided that he must be an impecunious noble second son with expensive tastes on his way to borrow more money from his elder brother, or at the very least that he was a wealthy plantation owner newly returned from the Americas and therefore unaware of the prevailing fashions on the Continent (which have already, thank heaven, set aside such ostentation as his costume advertised); now, however, forced to reevaluate my earlier conclusions, I was finding it most difficult to picture this romantic, aristocratic, if somewhat over-egged figure as a patient of the Marquis, let alone reconcile the sight of him with my recollections of the idiot Victor, scenes possessed of no greater quotient of nobility than might be wrung from the act of wiping the sputum off an old miser's lips, or else emptying his chamber pot (within which, often as not, the magpie had secreted everything from plaster saints to rusty nails to Roman coins, notwithstanding the expected and by contrast mundane substances for which the pot was intended by its makers).

4. Imagine how my surprise compounded, then, with a galloping pulse and trembling hand, a raised brow and

startled snort—these displays happily masked by the provident advent of our new driver into his box and his setting our distracted horse in motion, the animal manifesting precisely these same symptoms of amazement, or their equine equivalent, when its caretaker's whip sought to rekindle with its amnesiac hindquarters their old and intimate acquaintanceship—imagine, then, my surprise and surpassing discomfiture when the apparition brazenly sought my eye and addressed me by name, as though not a day had passed since the last occasion, where or when I could not say, he'd had cause to share a few words with the eldest son of his late master.

1. "Don Miguel," he said, unstuttering, "you must be finding this coincidence *a matter of no small astonishment*, and I would like to put your mind at ease. I would *like to*, I say, but I am unable to do so, for the circumstances of this meeting are indeed cause for disquiet."

5. I made clear to Victor that neither his presence nor this saturnine opening gambit, worthy of the worst sort of novel—upon which subject I have the misfortune to count myself an expert—were especially welcome on this of all days, and went on to ask if he might be able explain his changed appearance to my satisfaction in the time it would take us to reach our destination (not much more than an hour or two away), given that I had urgent business at Puységur and considered even a short delay

to be equally as unacceptable as undertaking said business while still in the state of unpleasant apprehension the combination of Victor's sinister reappearance and threatening prelude had encouraged in my already weakened organism.

2. "Don Miguel," he said, and I noted that his accent was a local, which is to say French one, far from the lopsided plunk of twenty years before, "not only will I do my best to satisfy your curiosity, but I have no intention of allowing you to go on your way before you've heard me out to the very last word, difficult though it will I imagine be for you to listen calmly and without prejudice to the fantastic tale I must now recount."

6. I made clear to Victor that I didn't care for the bullying tack our conversation had already taken—I, who, after all, if by proxy, had given him more than enough reason to show gratitude to myself or indeed anyone bearing my family name; numbering not least among these gifts the shelter of our ancestral home during his beastly adolescence (I mean before his miraculous transformation into a colonial beau)—and that I was by no means, even now, in my ill-health, a man to be trifled with, nor a man likely to suffer elaborate plots by *nouveau riche* ex-servants to divest him of what few reales he had left in this world (in case his performance was in aid of obtaining a loan) with anything approaching equanimity.

3. "Don Miguel," he said, and he shook a handkerchief from his sleeve with patrician grace, "of money I have no need, strange as this will sound to you, who know of my humble origins as a nursemaid to your father the sainted Don Félix, may he rest in piece. Would that money alone could assuage my suffering, or provide an answer to the terrible problem that so plagues me."

7. I made clear to Victor that there was little point indulging in additional insipid preambles and implored him to simply begin his story or riddle or request or whatever it was that he had set his heart upon plaguing me with, since our ride would be a relatively short one—though I wasn't myself familiar with that part of the country—citing the fact that the Marquis, whose hospitality I would soon enjoy, had told me that I would be expected for luncheon and that we could then stroll as an aid to digestion through his famous gardens before the no-less-famous sun went down over his vineyards; which scenario to me implied an early arrival, a deduction I fancied entirely reasonable and even clever.

4. "Don Miguel," he said, "in my experience, trips such as this, whether by horse, carriage, locomotive, rowboat, steamboat, galley, or shoe-leather never take any less time than is necessary for one traveler to tell another traveler the substance of his story, however prolix."

8. I was amused by this, and told Victor so—without abandoning the stern tone I had assumed from the start of our

unwelcome reunion, lest he mistake my chuckle for a sign of capitulation to his otiose ambush—taking care to point out that such was indeed the convention in badly written fictions, or indeed indifferently written ones (such as those I myself had executed and launched upon the blameless world like so many pebbles lofted at a Protestant), but that life as it is lived rarely makes such accommodations to our confessions, tall tales, imprecations, anecdotes, or lewd gossiping, however rapid our delivery, however precious to us the moral or plea we seek to decant into the pitiable ear of our patient interlocutor.

5. "Don Miguel," he said, "you cut, with your usual acuity, directly to the heart of the matter. You remember, I take it, what sort of creature I was when I was in service in your father's house. You were a kind boy, in those days, and I know that when you looked at me you saw not a gasping abortion but a noble soul imprisoned in the body of an unlucky homunculus: its Maker's hands having been withdrawn to tend to more promising projects before tongue, mind, and eye had been completed and conjoined in happy symmetry according to His usual—His by-and-large admirable—standard."

9. I made clear to Victor, albeit with some regret, that I had never once indulged in such happy speculations on his account, for I'd never once had cause to suspect that any such dignity of spirit resided in an individual so unworthy

of my close scrutiny—however badly such callousness must reflect upon my character then as well as now—but that, whether or not I or any other of his betters might then have guessed at his impending metamorphosis into the very figure of Man (writ large and robust, albeit with numerous dubious flourishes), it ought nonetheless to go without saying that however excellent the spirit of a fellow damned to poverty and ugliness, and however much pity he might provoke in his fellow *Homo sapiens sapiens*, it is no common occurrence for said excellence ever to make itself manifest in this world save through the base coin of allegory.

6. "Don Miguel," he said, "your bluntness does you credit: already you anticipate the gist of my terrible story, buried though it may be by my now over-fluent style of speech—so different, as you've noted, from that fumbling, distorted debasement of language that once issued from the dirty and subservient boy who slept under the roof of your father's house. But the penury of that unhappy child found itself alleviated long before my other, God-given chains, were loosed. Unbeknownst to yourself, or your brothers, or even your kindly mother, your father in one of his fits of lucidity bestowed a legacy upon me, drawing upon a secret account he had opened with a private bank. This was an establishment much relied upon by men of dubious morality known to be involved with the slave trade, or piracy, or worse, but which for this reason was, paradoxically, held to

be above suspicion by even such naturally suspicious men as these, and spoken of in the highest terms by those who had been lucky enough to be brought into the confidence of one of its brother patrons. Well do I remember the day when, dragged there by my own father, whose greed quite exceeded his familial affection where I, his youngest, was concerned—and always presuming, of course, that the rumors of my true, shameful parentage are without substance—I was made despite my treacherous tongue and brute manner to face the Director of this occult institution in order to sign with my own hand the papers releasing to me the generous bequest that soon made accessible the world of leisure and privilege into which God decreed that such as yourself are born."

10. I hastened to enumerate my many objections to Victor's increasingly audacious and even offensive story, reminding him that, for one, my father had died with so many debts that even Victor himself, whose remuneration had hardly been kingly, was turned out of our home without so much as a week's wages, once the creditors began to flock around the paternal casket; that, for another, I was no more born to privilege than any other scion of a family with no assets beyond a supposedly honorable name and a ramshackle, verminous house that fetched no more return through open auction than satisfied a single cheese merchant and three-quarters of a furrier; that, thirdly, my father was himself

a man of considerable crudity, and would be no more in possession of the arcane knowledge implied by a life of conspiracy, brigandage, secret fortunes, and deathbed bequests (to commendable but ostensibly uncouth beggar boys!) than a Porto whore might bed down every night upon the minutes of the Seventh Ecumenical Congress; and, finally, that whatever little luxury I might now seem to enjoy had been earned by what I am pleased to call the sweat of my brow, toiling in what must be the most ignominious trade to which a man of my education and sensibilities could be forced to turn, namely ghostwriting novels for dukes, cardinals, and other leisured parasites gifted with almost as little talent for literature as Victor himself, who seemed—I added with a certain zeal—to have burglarized the details of his manufactured biography from precisely the sort of trash I was at least spared the indignity of signing my own name to.

7. "Don Miguel," he said, "again, you have seen into the very heart of the matter. For am I not precisely one of those clients for whom you have written, at so many *reales* per thousand words, many of the books published (to much popular acclaim, if critical scorn) under my name, and to my great advantage? But do not tax yourself trying to remember which of your many customers I might be—I'm certain you don't know the family name I've adopted, and there must be plenty of other Victors to be found in your account book."

11. I lost no time in making clear to the man that there were, indeed, *no* Victors on my client list (to my certain knowledge), and that in any case—though I could not guess what he hoped to achieve with his persiflage—I hadn't been able to write a word for *anyone* in at least three years' time, this sorry admission demonstrating that we had not even begun to pry open the gate through which we might escape Victor's labyrinth of dissimulation; as such, there could be no doubt, I said, that he was nothing more than a singularly maladroit confidence man, whose plans to rob me or otherwise do me ill patently required the attentions of a ghostwriter of genius to revise into a workable draft.

8. "Don Miguel," he said, "see how our dialogue illuminates our situation. Allow me to ask, though I know it must be a sensitive subject, why you haven't been able to practice your purportedly ignoble trade these last three years? Is it not that, having suffered—let us say—a certain humiliation on the field of Eros, you found yourself unable to produce prose at the same volume, and with the same fluency, as you did in your youth?"

12. I made clear to him, controlling my temper (but for how much longer?) that I considered this implication—that virility and literary productivity have any connection whatever—to be of the same vintage and value as other notions peculiar to the schoolyard, for example that a poet

must starve, suffer, and pine in order to write just the right sort of drivel, or that a woman longed for but unpossessed is somehow more beneficial to one's imagination that one that is palpable, present, and personable.

9. "But Don Miguel," he said, "was it not on account of this very ailment that you first embarked upon this same journey, perhaps in this same carriage, to visit our mutual friend the Marquis de Puységur, and ask to receive his famous treatment? I am as certain of this as I am that your next words will be to deny that you have ever met the Marquis, or traveled this same route, or eaten at his table, or enjoyed the freedom of his pleasant gardens."

13. I made clear to Victor, seething, that I had never before met the famous Marquis of Puységur, that I had never before traveled this same route—citing my unfamiliarity, earlier, with the length of our already interminable ride to said Marquis's estate—and that I had never before eaten at this *or any other* Marquis's table, nor enjoyed the freedom of any gardens save those designated by kings and princes, with characteristic irony, as "public": for example, in Paris, that city whose characteristic accents Victor's speech had somehow absorbed over those same decades that I had descended to the level of a tradesman, while he, miracle that he was, had risen to the rank of, what . . . duke, viscount, baron?

10. “Don Miguel,” he said, “it’s true that I was able, at little inconvenience, given my yearly income, to purchase an insignificant and unobtrusive title for myself, in aid of ensuring that I would be able to move in the very best society, but your claim to ignorance regarding our false friend the Marquis is no more genuine than my store-bought peerage; which is to say, each serves its purpose well enough, and may be counted on to bear the weight of our and our friends’ credulity, but they do not issue from the bank of Nature—neither was minted by the screw press of true experience, but rather counterfeited, in your case by means of Animal Magnetism, and in mine by the writing of a bill of exchange and the addition of one innocuous line to the *Gotha*.”

14. I hasted to tell Victor that it was clear to me that whatever the source of the windfall he had enjoyed, the suddenness of his transformation from animalcule to angel had evidently deranged him, and *that*—I diagnosed—must be the reason for *his* visit to the Marquis; and, further, I announced that I would never be able to forgive our presumed benefactor for not having taken care that a perfectly normal (if anguished) man be spared the travail of sharing a coach with a lunatic, if only for the sake of his *sangfroid*, let alone safety.

11. “Don Miguel,” he said, “it’s only natural for you to become increasingly hostile as the truth of our situation is made clear. Since you can’t possibly feel threatened

by the strength of my—let us admit it—reedy and dilettantish arms, it must be the conviction with which I tell you my—or *our*—story that so alarms you, for I will persist in maintaining that this is not the first, no, nor the second, third, fourth, or even fifth time you've taken this journey to consult with the Marquis de Puységur. You have been in this coach almost as many times as myself, taken as I was to the Marquis when I attained the age of majority, as determined by the laws of our homeland. I was brought to Puységur by my loutish father in order that the Marquis might exercise his considerable powers (at a considerable price!) to transform me from the doomed creature you once knew to the—let us admit it—divine creature now sitting before you. Terrified, trembling, fouling myself, I was brought into the Marquis's garden and tied to his famous, ominous elm, which as you know has been magnetized by the Master over the course of his numerous experiments . . . all of which you too experienced (minus the incontinence, I hope?) when you were first bound to that selfsame tree, when you felt the similar if not selfsame twine itch upon your wrists, felt the tines of the bark beneath or behind you biting like temple spires into the skin of a toppling giant. In my case, seeing that I'd been safely immobilized, the Marquis began to expound upon his theories to my father, who was, it would seem, alarmed—hard heart or no—at my distress:

1. "'Modern philosophy, good sir,' the Marquis said, 'has admitted a plenum or universal principle of fluid matter, which occupies all space. As all bodies moving in the world abound with pores, this fluid matter introduces itself through the interstices, and returns backward and forward, flowing through one body by the currents that issue therefrom to another, as in a magnet, which produces that phenomenon that we call Animal Magnetism. I will now induce in Little Victor what the great Mesmer would refer to as "the crisis," which violent process shall expunge from his little body all those fluids causing the current imbalance in his being, and return him to a state of *tabula rasa*, as though newly born and primed to bear the imprint of the world (for good or ill). Except, in this case, we will not wait for happenstance to mark him with whatever impress Chance might in its blind groping toward the millennium cause to be stamped into his psyche. No, we shall give to Victor an opportunity received by no other soul in creation (outside of my care) save Adam. We shall *ask* him, in his trance, to give names to the things of the world, to tell us what he would like to become, and then we will endeavor to provide him with everything necessary to achieve the end sought by his perfected mind. He has, already, the means; in turn,

we shall give him the *learning*, the *vocabulary*, the *mannerisms*, and, most importantly, the *history*, or, more precisely, the *narrative*.'

12. "I remember my incredulous father, who, despite purchasing for me this remarkable prospect understood little better than I the processes by which it would be delivered, asking then where in perdition the Marquis, whatever his resources, could possibly acquire all of these things for his insignificant son.

    2. "'A little faith, good sir," requested the Marquis. 'There is a man, another of my patients, whose maladies I have been treating for years. He is not wealthy, indeed is of meager means. He must, therefore, barter for my services the use of his talents—equally meager, but sufficient for our requirements. He will, based upon your son's first utterances after the fever of his "crisis" has subsided, construct in the cause of Victor's improvement an entirely new life's story, not only granting your unfortunate son the *bearing* of a gentleman, but the *experiences*—which he will come to remember in preference to the first, foul text of his childhood—that give to such airs the substance of true nobility.'

13. "I remember my suspicious father saying then that he had associates of his own—and not a gentleman among

them—who, while they might not be so ingenious or erudite as those men in the Marquis's circle, could upon request furnish palpable evidence that their talents would nonetheless prove sufficient for providing the Marquis's exegesis with a learned commentary in the form of a sound cudgeling should this Magnetism business prove to be bullshit.

3. "'Well said,' admitted the Marquis, 'but I am undaunted. I have as much faith in my procedures as I do in the sun setting where and when I expect it to, or the River Gers freezing in winter. The very fact of your having come here with enough money to receive my miraculous treatment indicates to me that the process has already been a success—on yourselves, myself, and indeed on whichever other people it was necessary to influence in order to secure your son's unlikely legacy.'

14. "I remember my dubious father demanding an explanation for this outrageous claim, adding that the only supernatural influence he had heretofore noticed upon his life was that of God and his Host having been spiteful enough not to slay him in his cradle while still unburdened by sin.

4. "'Come, sir,' said the Marquis, 'it must even to a man of your paltry education seem extraordinarily unlikely that your son would be willed an enormous

fortune, and that this money would be disbursed in the manner you have related to me, by such absurd-sounding people, under such ridiculous conditions. I would wager that your lives have already begun to take on some of the serendipitous preposterousness of a serial novel. I do understand that it can be difficult for the layman to see the join between their life as it was lived before corrected by my expert hands and their life as it shall be lived thereafter, but I can assure you that the seam is as visible to me as, well, a setting sun or frozen river. Even the language with which we seem obliged to address one another seems to me a little affected, *de trop*, and in this I see the handiwork of my dear friend the author, who even now—believing himself a literary day-laborer suffering from impotence—sits in my study, drinking my cognac and ironing out the inconsistencies in the life of no less a personage than a member of the House of Obrenović, ruling body of the Principality of Serbia, who, to His Lordship's and our own great embarrassment, found himself involved with six duchesses simultaneously on account of a typo in an earlier edition of his sentimental education. As I've already explained to you, all creation is contained and preserved within a fluid matter, and as with any body of liquid, immersions, removals, upsets, overturnings, and maelstroms affecting one quarter come in time to affect all the remainder.'"

15. I hastened to make clear to Victor that it was becoming a greater and greater challenge to my naturally unsanguine temperament to hold my tongue throughout this fairy story, flattered though I was to be given a part of such prominence in it, having been made into something of a demiurge, capable of reducing the whole of creation to the standards of a penny-dreadful; further, excruciating though it was to choose only one objection from among the plenitude that plagued me, I told Victor that, were I to place myself in the role of *ad hoc* critic to his fiction, I would be obliged to point out the contradiction here between the Marquis's resolute belief in his own powers—his vaunted ability to tell at a glance where the Good Lord's *belles-lettres* left off and his Magnetical romances began—and his evident *un*certainty regarding the signs left by his, or *our*, meddling in Victor's life, "wagering" that the boy's fortune was his handiwork as though this were by no means a sure thing.

15. "Don Miguel," said Victor, "it was precisely this point that my poor father, overwhelmed by these startling and demanding concepts, next put to the Marquis, accusing him of building into his thesis the room to make a rhetorical *volte-face* should he be cornered at a later date. The unperturbed Marquis replied:

5. "'Why must you presume that I'm so irresponsible a practitioner as to employ these procedures against others without first having tested them on myself:

to be sure that they're safe, to see whether they may be relied upon, whether their benefits outweigh their dangers? Why must you presume that I am so ineffectual a conspirator as to allow myself to retain access to information that might expose even a tenth of the grand edifice that I have erected to the eyes of the mistrustful, the meddlesome, the *untreated*? No, good sir, I navigate my life or lives with neither foreknowledge nor memory of my actions or intentions as a Magnetist, finding my way purely by virtue of the God-given instinct I have retained—or perhaps had implanted?—for telling the difference between constructions natural and constructions no less natural but sweetened by my benign influence.'

16. "Did the Marquis mean to say, my father inquired, that he and I had been to Puységur already, before my luck had changed, to beg the Marquis's aid—and had been made to forget this?

6. "'Just so,' said the Marquis. 'It happens once or twice a year that someone unable to meet my fee makes a pilgrimage here to my chateau and thereupon gives me so bright and warm a display of their misery, stoking entreaty upon entreaty and sorrow upon sorrow, that it melts my heart—or else said heart is visited by some other chestnut beloved by our oblivious scribbler—and I take it upon myself to

arrange a cure not for the physical or psychical ailment that has brought them to my elm, but for the *penury* preventing me from curing their primary complaint (though, to be sure, poverty is the mother of all other ailments). I am not in the habit of giving handouts, nor are my patients likely to be the sorts of people to welcome pity—particularly after they begin receiving my treatments. They think too highly of themselves, or come to, and I think too highly of them as well.'

17. "My father then wondered to whom the money his son's late employer had willed to me actually belonged, allowing the Marquis to enjoy a moment's mirth at our expense:

    7. "'These unnecessary scruples,' he exclaimed, 'are merely a mild and, I guarantee, wholly treatable side effect of your prolonged affluence. But there's no need for anxiety. You ask whose money, "actually," you've been spending; I answer that there is no such thing as "actually," that "actually" went extinct on the day I set up my practice (if, indeed, "actually" ever "actually" existed, given the implausibility of even this initial step, for how could a man with my gifts be born, spontaneously, from Nature?). You must see that the instant it becomes possible to correct the fates of any gentleman or lady willing to submit

to my methods, in the hope of ameliorating some misadventure, neurosis, blemish, or regret, the imp is well and truly out of its bottle, and only an expert like myself has any hope of seeing the pattern of our plots as they are, or were—and even *that* knowledge is subject to tricks of the memory and the errors to which we are all heir. I am content in the knowledge that I might not have been born a Marquis, that I might "actually" be a toad or a grain of salt or a corpse or a washerwoman. It makes no difference to me, and it should make no difference to you.'"

16. Continuing in my role as critic of Victor's nonsense, the better to keep his perfidious fabrications at as great a distance from my person as our cramped conveyance would allow, I hastened to clarify to the man a point of rudimentary narrative logic that I felt had long since slipped through his inexpert authorial fingers, namely that there must be something *at stake* in order for a story to hold the interest of a reader or listener, and that his tale had already sacrificed all possibility of achieving this necessary tension with the introduction of the notion that there were *no* reliable incidences whatever in his fiction but only suppositions that could at a moment's notice be overturned by the unbelievable character of the Marquis—who, to make matters worse, was by his own admission completely at sea in his own "magnetic fluid," knowing neither up from down nor a cadaver from a condiment—such that, all in

all, Victor was positing a world without rules and without consequences and so without, in a word, *drama*; a world it would be impossible for anyone to care about, since no action on Victor's planet need have its consequence, no description its verisimilitude, no sequence of events a consistency that could not as easily be gainsaid and replaced with another, or another, or indeed all possibilities at once.

18. "Don Miguel," he replied, "as ever, you anticipate me: my incredulous father, finding the Marquis's latest sortie the least palatable yet, inquired if His Lordship could not then teach him how to fly, for he had long desired to visit the Holy Land, but was prone to terrible seasickness, and could not abide the dust of the road.

    8. "'There are limits to what we can accomplish,' sighed the Marquis, 'when it comes to the laws of Nature, as these have not yet yielded to me upon a certain few points of contention between my preferences and Hers. The reason for this is not a deficiency on the part of my technique, I assure you, but on the part of my desperately mundane scenarist, who despite being willing to delve into the most hackneyed conventions of his already degraded vocation without shame, despite his seeming eagerness to indulge in plots whose lurid convolutions would be sneered at by even the most venal sensationalist, still balks at composing material that might be said to transgress

> the boundaries of what he considers *realistic*—bearing in mind that what he considers realistic are secret societies and babies found exposed on cliff faces who bear birthmarks proving their right to the throne of Sweden. Having said that, however, you would not only begin to *believe* that you could fly, but that you were in the habit of visiting Heaven and playing patience with St. Eulalia, if I so desired. Whether you would actually rise into the air is a matter of conjecture, for the time being, but I will say that the basis of my practice is the notion that thought is not, as is commonly assumed, a *reproduction* of the world, which we keep inside our skulls, but rather its foundation. If a client appeared before me who would be contented with only *thinking* he could fly, to take your example, so long as everyone else he might come into contact with could be persuaded of this as well (myself generously included, for no extra charge), he would not be turned away from my door. The question, to my mind, would be whether or not such a widespread delusion wouldn't cause more harm than good to the subject; in that case, my professional ethics would not permit me to perform the procedure.'"

17. I hastened to declare that even such a self-evident ploy as this, for all its dexterity—imposing a few specious limits on the Marquis's omnipotence (along the lines of deciding,

for no reason but narrative convenience, that a ghost *may* be able to walk through walls but *may not* pass over running water)—couldn't undo the killing blow to causation already inflicted on Victor's narrative by his animating conceit, for how could such a potentate of the universe as our Marquis possibly come to be reliant on someone like myself: that is, upon the talentless drone I had been accused, if not without some justification, of being?

19. "Don Miguel," he replied, "my father, unlearned though he was, and probably intoxicated, took up this question as quickly as you have yourself, asking the Marquis why a man of His Lordship's wealth and background—be they authentic or merely an editorial imposition, as it were—should consider it necessary to employ a writer whose product he considered subpar, when presumably he could with his wealth hire any author alive. Moreover, why should his no less moneyed patients settle for inferior lives from an inferior pen?

   9. "'Modern physicians aren't expected to smelt their own instruments,' replied the Marquis. 'Neither can I be expected to invent my own scenarios for every person who comes to me in hopes of expunging a phobia, speech defect, *idée fixe,* humpback, clubfoot, class anxiety, or other deformity of the mind, body, or philosophy. I have not the time, nor the resourcefulness, to invent even *ten* such stories a year, let

alone fifty or a hundred. The same, I fear, applies to the first-rate authors I might employ or inveigle into my service; anyone sensitive or foolish enough to aspire to Parnassus would be too discouraged and exhausted to begin a project that they would in their right minds consider beneath contempt and then begin it anew between four and seven times a week, every week, year after year—assuming business is good. And even if *this* obstacle could be obviated, these authors of yours are all essentially crooks: they'll take your pay and still do *their* work instead of the task you've set them. (I say "essentially" because I speak of an fundamentally criminal essence in their constitutions that even my procedure can't entirely rout; or, rather, it *could*, of course, since little is truly beyond my capabilities, but what then would I have accomplished save transforming an author of talent *into* a hack rather than avoiding the use of a hack altogether?) Eventually, you see, a scenarist still harboring some *ambition* will always try to sneak something *gloomy* into his or her work, and this isn't what my patients come to me for. Excitement, yes; the giddiest of highs and the most lubricious of lows . . . but nothing *serious*, nothing *political*: our work is to soothe, not distract. So, my dear sir, what I need is a hack, the right sort of hack, with no self-respect to speak of; and fortunately for us all I found him very soon after first agreeing to give consultations to the public. He appeared at my door one morning in a freezing March, more a drowned dog than a man forlorn, soaked to the skin, having walked all the way from the nearest town for lack of money to hire a ride, having lost one shoe to a pucker in the road and his hat to the gale:

1. “““““Please, Sir,” he said;
2. “““““I can’t work, I can’t think, I can’t live.
3. “““““I’m incapable, a failure.
4. “““““No woman will touch me,
5. “““““not even for pay,
6. “““““and I couldn’t even afford to pay.
7. “““““I have gout in both big toes and thumbs.
8. “““““When I breathe, I cough;
9. “““““when I sleep, I kick
10. “““““ (and clench and cower);
11. “““““when I can think clearly, I think clearly shameful thoughts,
12. “““““except when they’re clearly frightful.
13. “““““What I eat burns me;
14. “““““and I can barely afford to eat.
15. “““““I’ve come to recognize that Nature never came to recognize me as one of Her own.
16. “““““My name was misspelled when entered into Her ledger.
17. “““““Or it’s since been erased,
18. “““““tampered with,

19. ““““or struck through,
20. ““““by parties unknown.””””

18. I made haste to inquire of Victor, with some hilarity, whether this threnody was meant to represent myself, his ill-starred carriage-mate, in my original, pre-Puységur state, and whether these complaints were really the best (meaning the most miserable) from which he could imagine a man such as myself suffering, even given a whole world of unhappiness (which is to say *this* one) to use as his model—whether it might not have been wiser to insert a miniature scenario at this point, told third (or was it now fourth?) hand, to explain my desperation; for example that my fall had begun in earnest when I'd caught my wife with another man, or, better, a woman, let us say a cousin or sister of mine, given that we're meant to be probing for ways to completely undermine any sense of *amour propre* in our protagonist (which is to say myself); more, I continued, warming to my subject, why not stir in a little business speculation gone awry, into which had vanished the last of the cash I'd realized on the sale of the rat-gnawed family home; this could even have been an investment into the mysterious private bank owned by my brother-in-law, a man of low character, which is to say the man married to the woman with whom my wife was now carrying on, and who I refused to inform about this betrayal of our respective trusts, out of a misguided sympathy (ignorant as I was of his schemes to cheat me)—or did little Victor believe in all hon-

esty that people, real people with blood and bones and skin and bowels, are "actually" brought to such desperate straits (*viz.*, knocking on a stranger's door during a cloudburst, begging for charity) by nothing more tragic than angst?

20. "Don Miguel," Victor said, finally demonstrating some impatience, "here at last you and my late father differ in your opinions. Impotence and gout and indigestion seemed to him more than enough justification for seeking supernatural aid, not least because—being an inveterate bibbler—my father suffered from all of these disorders himself. I am obliged to turn one of your criticisms back upon you: why would a man need such rococo woes as those you've suggested in order to be driven to desperation? You reveal your own sympathy for the gaudy, reveal most damningly the reasons why the Marquis has been able to make such excellent use of you; the lives of your bowel-men and bowel-women are (or *were*), per the world into which we were originally born, ruled by accretions of pettiness and chance, accumulated over generations—or so I must believe, based upon my admittedly flawed (because corrupted) memory of the days before Animal Magnetism undermined the pillars of Creation—and these pettinesses have led to great crimes and great accomplishments alike (assuming there is a difference). But *you*, my friend, forgive my saying it, wouldn't credit a little hunger or humiliation as sufficient to lead to a climax worth your attention.

You, Don Miguel, are as sick as you ever were—and I don't mean because you haven't had an erection in three years—sick at heart because you need all manner of erotic torments, terrible cabals, and encounters with oddities in cramped carriages to come to any kind of sociable accord with reality. Wives are, to a woman, faithless; all motives lubricious; all friends betrayers, all insight counterfeit . . ."

19. I hastened to disguise my perturbation at this latest turn in Victor's epic and so, stuttering, asked his opinion as to the Marquis's *motivation* in having set up his practice, since that too—motivation: a necessary element of drama, at least in my and Aristotle's insignificant philosophy—cannot exist inside a system where virtually any imaginable end is achievable before your character (the Marquis) even knows what it is that he desires, and in which every memory is perfectly malleable to his whims.

21. "Don Miguel," he replied, "we are, happily, back on track, because my father—for whom I still cannot find any forgiveness—did indeed anticipate this latest of your questions, next asking the Marquis, in much the tone one would employ with a child, what His Lordship hoped to achieve, in toto, with all his impressive work, and was he not worried about some eventual retribution being visited upon his august self, be it on the part of a rival Magnetist, the king, or even the Deity Himself?

9. "'My dear friend,' answered the Marquis, 'to whom do you think my putative rivals come with their petitions? I've set up many a Magnetist and counter-Magnetist, and they are all living in happiness and fulfillment believing themselves to be my most effective nemeses, plotting and counterplotting in perfect contentedness. And who, sir, do you think made the king into a king? Do you think that kingship is a *natural* phenomenon? But . . . better that you not know more. And while I hesitate to blaspheme before so pious a gentleman as yourself, God too may in time come to alight from his phaeton beneath my porte cochere and demand an audience with my distinguished self . . . only to discover that even He has been making use of my aid for quite some time already . . .'

22. "—and here the Marquis faltered and shook a handkerchief from his sleeve with patrician grace, waving it in front of his nose; I could catch the scent on it even from my place on the tree—

10. "'But, to answer your question,' he recommenced, 'with a question: what could it matter to you what I hope to achieve? The thoughtless answer would be 'a perfected world,' but in this too I feel my ghost-writer's hand at work, for what could be a more natural goal for a preening villain such as myself . . . or,

I should say, myself as he must see me? It's better said that *intention* is as obsolete as drama in our modern world, from which all limits to our capacity to reinterpret the evidence of our senses as we please have, delightfully, been removed. Let us satisfy ourselves with saying that my patients are a part of my *research*, and that I derive no little personal and unscientific gratification from seeing the beneficial effect I have upon the lot of humanity as a whole. As long as you get what *you* want (what you think you want, what I think you want), I will be happy. And you *will* get what you want—as will everyone, in time, when word of the services I offer has spread even across the ocean.'"

20. Immediately I crowed to Victor that neither he nor his Marquis had answered the question—which was natural enough, since even the Marquis had admitted there could be no satisfactory answer given the rules to which he claimed his millennium would adhere—and went on to point out the intrinsic flaw in *all* stories of this sort: to wit, that as soon as you've posited that the world in your work isn't the world as we know it but a counterfeit in which anything is possible, not only have you forfeited such bulwarks as drama, motivation, and conflict (with which we "meager" hacks must content ourselves), you find yourself obliged by this extreme measure to stake out farther and farther flung territory in order to invest the proceedings with any tension

whatever, eventually undermining the bases for your fantasy by attacking the mundane world to which your counterfeit domain has been set in opposition, positing that even *this* world (which is to say, our own, unliterary one) must itself be a fake or contrivance, stating that there must be another and marginally less-fake world beyond that, and another beyond that, ad infinitum, each presided over by its own paste-jewel divinity; and, moreover, the reader will come to *expect* every such subversion, refusing you even a whit of his credulity and coming to assume that whatever events you relate will by and by be overturned by the next revelation as a matter of course.

23. "Don Miguel," Victor said, "it gives me no pleasure to confirm that my father too seized upon this same point, if with a less elevated diction, and reminded the Marquis that a character such as the Marquis, not to mention the Marquis's vaunted abilities and accomplishments, did themselves rather resemble the invention of just such a drudge as His Lordship claimed to employ; the resemblance becoming that much more striking when the Marquis's own ambitions would appear to have been corrupted by the authorial turpitude of said drudge to the point that His Lordship could not himself be certain of their respective natures or pedigrees, which revelation had only served to return their conversation to its initial point, namely the question (then implicit, but now unequivocally put to the Master) of why exactly

it was necessary in the first place to tie his fool son to a tree, and how precisely the procedure was meant to work?

11. "Whereupon the Marquis had my father removed from the grounds, with the understanding that his presence would retard the Magnetism necessary to complete my transformation."

21. By this time, contrary to Victor's earlier reassurances or threats, I had to my great relief seen out my window the first green outcroppings of what I guessed must be the *real* Marquis's estate—cottages, fields, well-tended woods—indicating that my deliverance from narrative captivity was at hand, despite Victor's story having barely crested its first peak, let alone having entered its endgame.

23. "But Don Miguel," he went sternly on, seeing my excitement at the prospect of release, "the answer to my father's question is plain, as indeed is the answer to your question concerning the Master's motives. What the Marquis wanted, and wants, in reality—or what will have to pass for it given our indiscretions—are addicts, not patients; ladies and gentlemen who will return to him over and again, and who can now, having acquired his patronage, afford his services. After all, who among us could resist refining or revising our lives beyond the point

to which our initial fond wishes might bring us? Who, having received his heart's desire, would not soon tire of the spoils of his preliminary magnetization and develop new aspirations with which to torment himself?"

21. But surely, I said—finding myself a bit caught up, to my shame, in Victor's fragmentary fabrication—a man with the Marquis's purported powers wouldn't need money; why, then, hope to create legions of Magnetic Addicts when presumably a single patient would long ago have been enough to refashion Christendom in the Marquis's image?

24. "Don Miguel," Victor replied, "the answer is plain: a single patient was indeed enough to upset Creation, and the Marquis has never sought material gain. He has always been rich, was born rich—if we can say with certainty how any of us were 'actually' born. He seeks to create more addicts not for their business but because he wants *company* in his depravity, and an *audience* for his innovations—he is himself an addict, and in that capacity beyond hope: like a painter unable to resist adding new touches to a canvas already overdue at its first showing, he can't but submit to the perpetual allure of emending the world, and to that end, though perhaps without knowing it, his alterations, in concert with your strict if at best semi-conscious adherence to the tenets of the

cheap novelette, move we pawns—as well as himself!—inexorably toward disasters major and minor, which can only be combatted or erased by additional visits to the Magnetic elm. His reach is extended with each new patient, and each new patient is connected to however many thousands of other potential patients. As the Marquis improves one life, the means for that improvement must necessarily be stolen from another, and another, and another, creating an eternal debit, growing ever larger, more and more menacing, a debt that can never be paid, consuming all nations, and creating as it expands through each household the very conditions as will force an ever greater number of citizens to have recourse to Magnetism in order to find the means to survive, let alone live as they most desire . . ."

22. But surely, I sneezed, Victor had gained as much as anyone from this arrangement; why accost me, why disabuse me of my (*persisting*!) belief that I was and am only what I seem to myself to be: an aging and indigent also-ran visiting a most learned man—and for the first time, as I still maintained!—to beg some relief for certain niggling if awkward vexations?

25. "Don Miguel," he said, "the answer is plain. I am tormented by the knowledge of what's been done to you—I and so many others have profited from the use, dis-

grace, grief of the only man who can never fully benefit from the Marquis's Magnetism, and can never even be allowed to hear the true facts of his own life (not that he would or does believe them when they're told to him . . .). It would be one thing for you to give us everything that you have given *willingly*, but it's quite another for the Marquis to use you as a lamp does its oil, or, perhaps more appositely, a pen its ink. You have given to half of Europe its history, its wealth, its worldliness or piety, its lusts or chastities—and yet not only have you never been cured of the worries that first brought you to Puységur; you haven't been able to take even that small gratification in your work as is owed the meanest pavement artist turning out a nicely chalked cheekbone. I have intercepted you today for no other reason than give you the very thing the Marquis once gave to me, and to all of his clients save you, who dragged himself to the chateau asking for help and in return lost his soul: a choice."

23. I pointed out, in better humor now that our journey was ending, that Victor's saintly conscience might have been better balmed by further indulgence in the Marquis's Magnetism, and that this resort would after all be the better palliative—would it not?—since it would erase the memory of his ever having felt its pricks in the first place . . .

26. "Don Miguel," he said, "I have good reason to believe that I have *already* availed myself of further treatments

at the elm to accomplish just this; I can only speculate that I am afflicted with an integrity so formidable that the Marquis is unable to overwrite it; or else, more plausibly, that, among your many other faults as an author, you lack the imagination to point me down a different path, so wedded are you to the scenarios with which you've plied your trade, instructing us as they do that crimes must lead to guilt, which leads to repentance, tragedy, redemption, and so forth. It may be that some part of you recognized me from your father's service when I appeared before the Marquis as a client, and that this higher part of your intelligence grasped onto that familiarity in desperation (always presuming that this too is not one of the Marquis's contrivances), seeking to free yourself from your submission to the will of the Marquis by employing me as a defense mechanism, a counterplot, tirelessly and against your own will fighting to contain the infection represented by the influence of our benefactor."

24. The sound of our horses' hooves clacking over cobbles now signified to me that our journey was winding to a close, and the relief of this was twofold, in that it meant not only clemency as far as the likelihood of any supplementary imprecations on Victor's part, but that those elaborations I would have to tolerate nonetheless, over the remaining minutes of our ride—until at last our driver climbed down and opened the carriage door for me—were muffled and

occasionally, wonderfully, incomprehensible beneath the clamor.

25. Why not, I hastened to ask, little caring whether Victor could hear me, half hoping that the rest of our trip might be taken up with our calling "What? What?" at each other, why not, I asked, challenge the man to a duel, since you are of comparable ranks; or, better still, poison his wine, or hire men to accost and murder him on some back road, or shoot him in the head when you next present yourself for treatment; why not today, why not here and now do away with this great threat to humankind, not to mention dramatic tension; or were the Marquis's powers so great that he could mesmerize a bullet in its flight, convincing it that it's only a swallow, or a dust mote, or an airborne seed?

27. "Don Miguel!" Victor called, over the clattering, the catcalls of the carriage's rusty springs, as though trying to make himself heard over a great lunar gulf, not a span so tight that only a child could have easily maneuvered through and over our legs, "The route out of our impasse is simple, so simple that Puységur himself could not, in his intricacy, conceive of it; so simple that you, my dimwitted friend, could not have anticipated it for him and thus remove it, and me, from the plot. It comes as no surprise that you favor violence as the means out of our predicament, since this is how you believe the world must work, and how you've *made* it work, and

been influenced by it in turn. Yet I believe it took a mind like my own to hatch it—a mind never entirely divested (by accident, or through your own flawed design?) of its brutish scruples. It hasn't, in any case, the Marquis's smell about it, so I allow myself to have some confidence that it wasn't he who first gave it me; such doubts are his greatest weapon, and we must not yield to them. My solution is absent of finesse, you see, or indeed the consideration due one gentleman by another; it has all the refinement of knocking over an inkwell with your elbow, but will be quite as efficacious in effacing our common errors. Lean in close to me, my friend, so that I can speak it in your ear, for we can't know how much of this meeting, how many of our words, might already be contaminated by the influence of our sponsor, and neither can we know how much of what we take for granted in our lives might collapse without the dam you have built to keep the river of what you call causality at bay; how the current, freed, might wash back and change us before you ever manage to carry through my plan, simply by your intending it; might wash back and change you before you have a chance to leave this carriage, before you think to buy a ticket for this journey, before you wake up the day before yesterday having dreamt of murdering a man in a green, wooded, solitary place; before your father dies, before you learn to speak—how even the means we have of communicating with one another might vanish (and good riddance to them, in all frankness): our intelligences, sentiments, the circumstances of our conversation, even the breath in our lungs. Do you not anticipate my suggestion? You are the only person alive who can effect it. The carriage will stop, the driver will open the door and put a step beneath it; you'll emerge, and be greeted by the Marquis's footmen, who will escort you to your usual room, where the paper is kept, and the bound volumes of our lives, and the battered divan on which they let you sleep, when you can't help but sleep, slumped.

"Listen carefully, for this is what you must do . . ."

ACKNOWLEDGMENTS

Several stories in this volume make use of short quotations from other works, including the following:

"Ten Letters" contains some words from Henry James's *What Maisie Knew*.

"On the Furtiveness of Kurtz" contains appropriations from the *Epic of Gilgamesh*; vol. 25 of the *Missionary Review of the World* (January to December, 1902); Blaise Cendrars's *Trans-Siberian*; and Gerald of Wales's *De instructione principis*.

"Illness as Metaphor" contains passages from Robert E. Howard's "Black Colossus," as well as John Gardner's *The Art of Fiction*.

"Delete the Marquis" contains a passage from the anonymous pamphlet *Wonders and Mysteries of Animal Magnetism Displayed*, 1791.

The author gratefully acknowledges the magazines and anthologies in which some of the stories in this volume were first published, largely in different form:

"The Dandy's Garrote" originally appeared in *The Official Catalog of the Library of Potential Literature*.

"Forkhead Box" originally appeared in the *White Review*.

"Illness as Metaphor" originally appeared in *VLAK*; a shorter version, under the title "My Diagnosis," also appeared in *Harper's*.

"The Knack of Doing" originally appeared in *The Coming Envelope*.

"On the Furtiveness of Kurtz" originally appeared in the *Brooklyn Rail* online.

"The Sinces" originally appeared in *Golden Handcuffs Review*.

"Ten Letters" originally appeared in *Anemone Sidecar*.

"The Terrible Riddles of Human Sexuality (Solved)" originally appeared in *Mad Hatters' Review*.

Thanks too are due this volume's editor, Aaron Kerner, as well as M. S. Atwell, John Brandon, Scott Eden, Kay Grossman, A D Jameson, Anna Keesey, Zachary Lazar, Marshall N. Klimasewiski, Rebecca and Sara Malgeri, Joy Williams, and Paul Winner.